THE ANCIENT SECRET OF

CLOVEN HILL

JANE YEADON

with

Darcey Alexander, Scarlett Britain, Zack Carroll, Aleysha Chan, Izabella Cruickshank, Alice Culley, Ella Fullerton, Lewis Giffen, Sophie Howard, Marcus Jamieson, Freya Kendrick, Eilidh Mackenzie, Macy McLean, Ellen Manson, Bethany Mcghee, Ewan McRae, Lauren Munro, Grant Napier, Angus Robertson, Daniel Robertson, Abbie Theman, Harriet Wheeler, Eryn Wright, Elle Anderson, Evie Barry, Holly Cumming, Eva Esslemont, Abi Ettles, Abigail Ferry, Olivia Gray, Cate Hartley, Natasha McNaught, Kate Millar, Demi Ward, Alina Foerster, Bruce Burns, Logan Ferguson, Marcus Glen, Aiden Harvey, Fergus Kenyon, Joshua Kippax, Rory Derbyshire-Laing, Murray McGregor, Ben Meacher, Arran Netherwood, Joseph Owen, Harley Sharp, Arron Tester and Alec Williamson.

Proceeds from the sale of this book go to
UGANDA AID PERSON TO PERSON
Scottish Charity No. SC036939

ACKNOWLEDGEMENTS

Thanks to webmaster and spiderman Tez Watson, Mark for 'ruggabug', Joanne for the joy of handstands, Anne Reid, Sara Neil and Nigel Sleaford for not in the least resembling teacher Miss Crowe in the book, but without whose help, ideas and inspiration The Ancient Secret Of Cloven Hill would not be what it is.

CONTENTS

October 2015

Anderson's Primary School is proud to have been involved in putting together this book.

It has been just wonderful to have been part of a project that let the children explore their imagination and learn about story writing in such a fun way.

M. Mooney

Maureen Mooney
Head Teacher

1: A RUDE AWAKENING

YOU MIGHT NOT BELIEVE in witches and snotty-nosed monsters with red eyes, feet smelling of old cheese and long black toe nails. Still, if you heard slithering, scraping and scratching sounds outside your window on a dark and stormy night, you might imagine that something pretty horrible was trying to get into your bedroom.

You'd probably be pretty brave about it but, in the circumstances and land of hills, heather, haggis and monsters, it was making eight year old Burns McRae sweat. His mouth was dry and his heart was thumping so hard, it should have drowned out the noise.

Yet, rising above it and sounding like a starving fiend, the wind raged, banshee–screamed, shouted and whooped round the family home. And even above that, came that odd scratching noise. And it was terrifyingly close.

Tap tap.

'Ruggabug!' he whispered.

It was his best word for a crisis. He'd made it up. It saved him using bad language and having to pay a fine into the family swear box: a nasty little tin with a slot in it. He knew he was the only one who ever put money in it.

It was so unfair.

He twiddled his toes to check that at least there was something he could count on. Twiddle, twiddle. Eleven! Yup - six on one foot, five on the other.

Burns found this handy for counting but, in case he grew any more, his mother had taken him to see a doctor.

'It's unlikely. Now please hurry and put your trainers back on,' he'd said, wrinkling his nose. As he threw open the surgery window, he took a lungful of fresh air, before going on, 'You never know when another spare might come in handy, so, Burns, you mustn't worry.'

He meant to reassure but in Burns's experience, adults often meant the opposite to what they said. He'd been happy enough until the visit. Now he thought, bloomin' nuisance of a doctor. What does he care I couldn't get trainers to fit or I'd have to learn a different way of counting?'

No wonder he was always checking his feet. He twiddled the eleven again. Good – no new arrivals and all working to his command. At least he'd still control over somethings.

For a moment, the noise stopped.

'Phew!' He uncurled his toes. 'Maybe the monster's gone to Rosie's window. She'll soon sort it out with yon cassowary kick of hers.'

He thought about his big sister. If she got mad or frightened, she never swore. No. Not Rosie! She'd learnt to kick like the big bird called a cassowary after a visit to a zoo when she saw one shoot its leg out backwards. There was a resultant bang and splat with the poor thing that had been in its way getting loads of bruises to replace its lost blood and guts.

A backward kick hadn't worked for Burns though. His legs couldn't be long enough. When he kicked backwards, he fell forwards. He rubbed his bum, still sore after the ground-landing he got after trying out a few shots.

He thought about the swear box. It was an unjust world. Look at his parents! Neither of them ever-ever-ever seemed to put money in the dratted box even when his Dad, after dropping a hammer on his toe, should have.

He dived under the bed clothes, covered his ears and as the noise started again, whispered, 'Ruggabug!' 🐾

2: FACING DANGER

H IS PARENTS AND ROSIE MUST BE DEAF! If Burns had had a mobile, he'd have phoned for help, but this was a time before anybody had one. He could have shouted, but all that would do would let that thing outside, know he was inside. For the moment, it probably wasn't sure.

Tap tap.

Accepting that it was never going to go away, all Burns could do was shut his eyes and accept his fate.

'Goodbye, World,' he said, screwing his eyes close–tight. But that now gave him something else to worry about. What if they never opened again? Even if he was only half-eaten, he'd be doomed.

'Doomed!' He tried the word out and thought about bumping into everything and everybody with his eyes stuck-shut. He didn't much care for their colour and tried to console himself thinking, that at least it would stop his Ma's friends always going on about them.

'Oooh's he's got lovely green eyes,' they'd say before falling to the ground as if fainting in admiration.

It was so embarrassing but Rosie was worse. All she did was laugh.

'Be glad they were speaking about your eyes,' she'd said. 'If it had been about your ears, they'd have said they were like,' pausing for a moment, she hopped twice, then jeered, 'bonny jug-handles, 'cos they are. Great big ones, and as for your eyes, well - they're more like traffic lights. They go red when you're in a rage.'

Maybe she was right. Just thinking about Rosie made his eyes burn. In case they went on fire, he shot them open. Phew! Just another danger averted, but just in case of any problems, he went without blinking. He managed to completely cover his ears with his hands. They were either growing or his ears were shrinking, but still he could hear the noise so he plugged his fingers hard into both ear-holes.

'Ouch. That's sore.' He curled into a ball, longing to be a thousand miles away and safely away from a thing that was bound to eventually get in. It was just a matter of time and surely by this time, it must be starving with cold and worse, by now, ragingly starving.

'Ruggabug!' he croaked.

13

'Whooooh!' Carried on a cold draught, a new moaning noise came into the room.

Risking a peep over the duvet, Burns muttered, 'Go away. I'm not frightened and stop blowing on my face.' He touched his chilled cheek. 'Uh! I think you've frozen it. You horrible thing – you've given me lockjaw.'

He waggled his chin and stuck out his tongue. 'Well, maybe not. Phew!'

When nothing ghastly happened, he looked about.

'Aaargh!' He sat bolt upright.

'Somebody's left a bit at the top open,' he shouted and punched his pillow, 'and that somebody's Ma of course! She's always going on about fresh air. You'd think she'd worry that her one and only son might freeze to death if not swallowed alive.'

He bit his lip, drawing blood. It tasted horrible. How can vampires like that? He thought for a moment. Well, actually, the window was only a little bit open. It would have to be a very small monster to get through it.

His voice sounded faint but clear. 'Ha! You'll never get in. I bet you're far too big.'

Heart beating loud, he waited for a response but only the scratching sound persisted. Shivering, he looked about. Then he felt the same relief that he got when his Ma said he didn't have to finish his lumpy porridge.

'Silly me,' he said and kicked himself – but gently. A bruised leg was hopeless if he'd to make a quick escape and of course it wasn't a moany old ghost. It was just a draught sneaking in from the storm, whistling through the window and strong enough to make the curtains move. They swayed as if doing that stupid dance his parents called the waltz. The very thought of it made him groan. In terms of the fear-factor, momentarily, the evil thing lurking outside, now took a back seat.

Honestly, thought Burns. What had he to look forward to anyway? If he survived this terror, what waited for him was the misery of Saturday night's Take the Floor on the radio with his Ma and Dad dancing to its music. They seemed to think that having them crashing around in the sitting room to the sound of Drummond Trot's band was better fun than watching Dr Who on telly.

It was unbelievable. He was sure they just did it to annoy him. Burns creased his brow and scratched his nose. Mortified, he thought about the worrying moments when friends might call. They'd see his parents waltzing as if this was normal behaviour.

He wondered how they'd feel when they find out he'd been eaten alive by a monster. Instead of having that silly jazzing about, they'd be sorry alright. Unfortunately, thinking about his unpleasant future brought him back to the present.

His heart pounded. It felt so sore knocking against his chest wall he wondered if it was trying to escape. Maybe looking for somewhere safer. The hole it left would give the monster the chance to take up residence inside him. It'd pretend everything was normal. How would anybody know?

'Spect my bloomin' parents would be too busy waltzing to notice.' He tapped his head. 'Only you would know the difference.'

He shuddered. He began to fancy that the curtains looked threatening. He tried to stop his imagination but it was no use. Any minute now he could see them coming adrift, advancing, then, quick as a flash, leaning over and smothering him. Burns took a deep breath. With so much evil about, he had to take action.

Ruggabug! 🕷

3: ACTION!

CAREFULLY, HE INCHED ONE ARM ALONG THE BED. Slowly, slowly it moved and down the side until at last his fingers reached the floor. Then, like a scuttling spider they moved, desperately searching, before they closed over the hilt of his Rapid Response Rapier.

It was a Sound and Light sword. Thank goodness he'd kept it close.

His trigger finger hovered over the sound control button until he remembered his mother's words. 'That bally thing's loud enough to waken the dead.'

Burns reckoned he'd problems enough without a zombie alert and anyway coming from his mother, such a comment was a bit rich.

'She makes twice the racket when her Duff Pipe Band group of wifie-friends come to practise here,' he muttered. He tried not to think about them, but still they stuck in his mind.

'Let's raise the roof!' they'd cry, fingers running over the chanter bit of their bagpipes. With cheeks blown out and kilts stretched over their fat bums they'd march about the sitting-room.

'Ma! They're like tartan hamsters on parade,' Burns had said, not really joking.

'You may laugh but at least they've the figure for kilts,' she'd replied and for once her son was grateful that he was small and thin with knobbly knees and a foot with six toes. Wearing a skirt would be the ultimate disgrace.

Ma's chums were all built big but the roof stayed in place whilst their racket moved non-players out of range and Dad McRae to the bike-shed where there was no swear-box.

It just proved sound could be a useful weapon but Burns thought he'd use his sword's light-switch first. It'd been very effective when he'd tried it on Rosie. He remembered pointing it at her and for a moment forgot his present fear. She'd gone red. 'I'm telling Ma!' she'd cried, then went speechless.

He wasn't sure how many brains she'd had to begin with but, with the sword's beam strong enough to fry them, he'd been a bit worried

17

when she didn't talk again. Not for a full five minutes!

Still, that should be enough time to get that evil, scrabbling enemy backing off so that he could decide on his next move.

He drew the sword towards him then stabbed at the red button on the hilt etched with skull and crossbones.

'Ruggabug!' he muttered and tried again, but nothing happened. Rosie must've pinched the batteries and it certainly wouldn't work without them. He ground his teeth. She'd had her revenge but how could anyone expect him to now operate as saviour of the house without light or sound?

'Uhhh!' He treated himself to some swear-box words, momentarily pleased his parents weren't around to make him pay for them. He toyed with the sword blade. It still might have its uses. Grasping it, he swung his legs out of bed.

Then, with the encouraging thought that if he survived tonight, he'd kill his bloomin' sister, he circled the pile of clothes he always left in the middle of the floor and tiptoed towards the moving curtains. As they parted, a pale sliver of dawn's light showed. Morning mustn't be far away.

Mustering all his courage, Burns grasped the curtains.

'Don't do it. Just get Ma and Da!' pleaded voices inside his head. Ignoring them, he tore the curtains apart, flung open the window to its full height, stuck his head, shoulders and arms out, then, whirling the sword like a helicopter, cried, 'Ruggabug!'

There was a roar like something angry and gathering speed. He felt an intense pain and then, in agony, found, he was trapped. 🐛

4: A BRAVE ACT

THE WINDOW HAD CRASHED DOWN. Its weight pinned him and now that he was stuck half in with his shoulders and head, half out, that horrible something was poking and sliding all over his face instead.

Burns blinked, waiting for the final attack. But, then, he felt a surge of relief. It might be sore but it was relatively harmless. It was only the storm-tossed branch of a nearby ash tree. And it wasn't a monster and he didn't believe in witches. Well, not really, but balancing on the branch was something that could've belonged to one. It really was astonishing. His green eyes met the same coloured ones of an enormous black animal with the longest white whiskers Burns had ever seen on a cat.

All that perfecting balance on her broomstick would have explained why this one managed to stay on the swaying branch. Of course, its great big claws - huge and dug into the wood might have helped.

Burns hoped that this wasn't the one the folk in Inverspurtle, his hometown, spoke about. Very few had seen it, but those who did, swore that it had brought them bad luck.

And maybe they were right. As the cat fluffed up to an even bigger size, arched its back, spat, lashed its tail then disappeared, Burns felt something odd at his feet.

He squirmed his toes, counted them. Yup - still eleven but now there was a bit of tickling and occasional nibble. Maybe he was going to be eaten alive after all.

'Ruggabug.' The wind snatched his voice and threw it back and down his throat.

It'd begun to rain, the drops falling like the tears Burns was fighting against.

'Yuck! Brose! You silly dog, don't you know he's got cheesy feet? Come here!'

Even if she hadn't spoken, Burns would've known it was his sister as a smart smack landed on his bum.

'Ha! Gotcha! What a target!' She chuckled, then went on, 'An' it serves you right. You were making such a racket, you woke me and Brose.'

More tears, but, now, of frustration, welled up. Between being squashed to death and this latest insult, all Burns could do was swallow hard and inwardly seethe.

Struck by his silence, Rosie advanced, pinging her fingers on the elastic of his Superman-pyjamas. 'I see you're in a sticky situation,' she said, 'or are you just hanging about?'

Despite a red mist of rage descending, he managed to sound reasonable. 'Lift this bloomin' window, will you?'

'Say "please," and I might.'

His uncaring sister did a handstand beside the window allowing him to see just her face - if upside down. It wasn't an improvement. It made him feel giddy.

'Cool! Your face is really white.' A note of admiration crept into her voice, 'and your freckles so stick out, you look like a rock bun.' She landed back on her feet, grasped the handles of the window, then shot it up with the ease of a shot putter. Rosie's muscles were very effective.

'There!'

Burns fell back into the room. A small wiry-haired brown dog gave up on his feet and licked his face instead. Her stubby tail whirred like a propeller.

'Yuck! Brose - you've got dog's breath and you've been rolling in something horrid.'

He wasn't being unkind. There were many things Burns loved about their dog and, in particular, the fact that she didn't mind criticism. This was obvious from the way she now lay wriggling, looking cute and not minding that she smelt of long dead fish.

There were times when Brose could make Rosie seem even human, but now, kneeling beside their dog, she was more like a clucking hen. 'Och, ma wee pet. Somebody must've left the outside door open and you sneaked out. Honestly, you're such an escape artist and you found old bonie wonies and took them back for a good chew, didn't you, you wee scamp.' She wagged a finger. 'And you know Ma doesn't want you in my bedroom. But you get lonely if you're not sleeping with My Little Ponies in their stable in my room, don't you?'

Burns could never figure out how nice Rosie could be to Brose whilst she always gave him a hard time. Still, she had rescued him from being sliced in two and he was grateful.

'You saved me from death,' he said, rolling his eyes. 'If you hadn't come, one half of me would be here and the other splattered on top of the paving slabs down below. Think how everybody would feel at my funeral. They'd have to mourn over two coffins.'

'Tch! You're so into drama, Burns. At some point somebody would have come and rescued you. Da probably. He wouldn't want your blood, guts and brains all over the slabs he's so proud of laying.'

'S'pose.' He felt weak and drained and having a sister who was such a pain, didn't help. 'You bloomin' well nicked my sword's batteries,' he said. 'You keep doing it and it's so annoying.'

'What! That rubbishy thing?'

Rosie had red hair. As she shook her head, her curls bounced, looking like rusty bedsprings. 'It's ready for the bin. Anyway, me an' Midge were fed up. Nothin' to do this weekend, so we're planning an adventure and we need batteries for the metal detector.'

'That's mine too.'

'S'not.' Voice raised, Rosie jabbed him. She might have thin arms but her elbow was seriously mean.

Brose whined. She loved humans but hated when they rowed. What tail she had, she managed to tuck down. Then she slunk out of the room.

'See what you've done! You've upset the dog... and if you shout anymore you'll wake Ma and Da.'

'No I won't. Even if they're downstairs I can still hear them snoring.'

Rosie wrinkled her nose. It was quite long and very sensitive to smells. 'Mind, if they get a whiff of Brose, they'll be up and raging she's been let out. Then we'll be for it.' She made a face. 'It's even a bit whiffy round here - but that's probably your trainers. They really do stink. That window needs opening again.'

'I'm not going near it, ever-ever again.'

'You softie!' Rosie scoffed. She got up and, taking one of Burns's trainers sitting on top of his clothes pile, used it to jam open the window.

Morning was fast approaching. The light was strengthening, the wind had dropped and a fine drizzle of rain softened birdsong. All was peaceful until the garden gate creaked opened.

It must be the paper boy.

Brose was out again, presumably busy looking for more bones, but must've stopped when she'd noticed a caller or maybe she'd seen the black cat.

'Grrh!' She could sound quite fierce when she wanted to. The children didn't worry. She'd never caught or bitten anything and every visitor would be welcomed as she collapsed in a heap of wriggling joy at their feet. Anyway, the paperboy was used to her and if he did see her would whistle before calling out, 'Hey, Tiger!'

This morning there was no such friendly greeting. Made curious by the silence, Burns was drawn to the window and glimpsed a black tail disappearing under a bush. Cat? Should be a sign of good luck: but not this time.

'Ruggabug! It's Picker Macsnott. The biggest bully in town!'

Horrified, he saw a huge boy with greasy black hair slouching toward the patio, trailing a newspaper bag behind him.

Suddenly, seconds after Picker raised his boot, there was a heart rending howl. Brose sailed through the air. For a moment she looked like a small rocket, but then she crash-landed in a tiny heap onto a paving slab.

Appalled, the children stared down: saw their beloved dog lying still.

There was no way she could have survived that kick. She must be dead! 🐾

22

5: A THREAT

IT SEEMED LIKE A LIFETIME, but it was only seconds before Brose moved. It was just a little flicker but at least she was alive. She lay on her back, whimpering and just able to raise a small submissive paw. Picker raised his boot again.

A blackbird flew away, scolding, perhaps warning of Brose's impending doom. Crows, rooftop-sentinels flew into the air. They sounded like they were cawing, 'Death, death.' For a moment Picker seemed to be listening as if they were singing his favourite song, then over the sound of Brose's whimpers and the gate squeaking to and fro, a blood curdling yell split the air.

Rosie had flown to the garden. Her legs were a blur of movement and she was shouting. Her words might have added lots of money to the swear box but at least they stopped Picker's boot.

From bitter experience Burns knew she meant Cassowary business. A leg, mean as her elbow, shot out, dealing a killer blow to Picker's thigh. His boot met fresh air instead of Brose. He toppled under pressure of Rosie's attack as Burns flung open the window. He fired one of his trainers at Picker.

'Ruggabug. And right on the mug!' He shouted, delighted.

'And serves you right,' cried Rosie, snatching up Brose before running back inside. She slammed the door behind her with such force, the whole house shook.

Picker looked up, then got off the ground slowly, rubbing his head in disbelief. His eyes blazed like red-hot coals in a white face with a chin so sharp you could dig a grave with it.

'I'll get you for this, McRae - Muck,' he snarled. 'That's the last time I'll ever do anyone a favour.'

He pulled out a long knife from his pocket. 'Anyway, paper rounds are rubbish.' He caressed the blade with a grimy finger, twisting his face into something that might have been a grin if he'd been anybody but Picker.

The sun caught on the blade so that it glittered like a shaft of light. Brandishing it with one hand, he yanked a paper out of his bag with the other.

It was the Inverspurtle Weekly and Da's favourite weekend read. Picker swung it round his head then cackled, 'Ha ha! And here's twice your weekend reading.' He held the paper up as if to read it then, with a swift slice of the knife, cut it in half. 'Barrrgain!'

As both pieces fell to the ground he stamped on each then turned on his heel.

'An' I'll be seeing you soon, ye wee runt,' he shouted.

As he left, he banged the garden gate shut so hard, sparks flew from it like fireworks. 🐝

FOR THE LOVE OF MIKE!' shouted Da McRae. He'd burst into the living room where Burns now sat with Rosie nursing Brose. Their father's legs were spaghetti white and so long they stuck out miles from under his dressing gown. He was running fast in circles. 'Can a man no get a bit of peace?'

' Da-a-a-d! Brose's had a terrible experience,' wailed Rosie, wiping her nose on the back of her hand. 'It was all Picker Macsnott's fault. He nearly killed her.'

'What?' Her father stopped his circuits for a moment to stare at Rosie who went on, 'But, Da, don't worry. I've found her pulse and she says she's going to live. I've told her she doesn't know how lucky she is to be alive. Me an' Burns,' she continued, poking her brother hard, 'dunno why he was delivering papers. He was happier kicking our wee dog to death.'

Hearing her name, Brose cocked her ears.

'See Rosie? She's listening to see if you've got the story right,' said Burns. 'She's a very brave animal.'

He wished he could feel the same about himself. Wait till Da heard about his Inverspurtle! He always read it in the bath. It was his idea of a relaxing Saturday morning treat. He'd go mental especially when he found the paper in half and soaking wet before it ever went near taps. This was one dreadful Saturday. Ruggabug! It was even worse than a day of full-on country dance music.

Meanwhile Ma McRae had arrived. On hearing the story, she narrowed her eyes. 'Well that's a bit of excitement,' she said, 'and it's certainly got us all up. If I get that laddie I'll wring his neck.' As if practising, she pulled her dressing gown belt and tied such an expert knot, Burns thought that as well as protecting him she'd be handy as an anchor person in a tug of war team. Her weight would help too.

'And you two look as if you've had a bit of a fright.' She checked her huge watch. It was a sweetie pink which clashed so violently with her camel coloured dressing gown, you could get a sore head just looking at it.

But it didn't seem to bother Ma as she said, 'You could do with a nice treat. I'll make you some of my nice bannocks. You know how you love them.'

'No!' Everybody shouted. Da did another floor circuit. All this and not even the Inverspurtle to cheer him up!

'Don't be silly. You'll need something to keep your strength up and grow bonny,' Ma insisted and strode off to the kitchen.

Burns groaned. He certainly did want to grow – but not by the bannock method. At least this was something that all the family but Ma agreed on. She was such a terrible cook there was more risk of food poisoning than the necessary spurt of growth that would be necessary for dealing with the mean machine that was Picker.

Brose jumped off the sofa. With her stumpy tail held high she was apparently well on her way to recovery. Forgetting everything but her stomach she trotted through to the kitchen to investigate the din heralding Ma's culinary efforts.

By the sound of things, progress on the bannock front was well underway as Ma gave a triumphant yell. 'Gotcha! A bluebottle was fancying having a taste – but don't worry, I caught him with my fish slice. Now don't any of you disappear. I'll be through with your food in a minute.'

The door bell rang.

'What if it's Picker,' worried Burns, 'come to finish me off.'

7: PLANS!

IT WASN'T PICKER. Burns breathed again.

'Midge and Andy! Come in come in,' said Ma. She slapped down a tray-load of leaden, fly-splat garnished grey lumps onto a small table which Burns used to practise flying from until his Da shouted 'Careful!' making him misjudge his flight path and fall, twisting his ankle.

His mother stepped back to look at the tray in approval. She said, 'You two are just in time for a bit of munch as well so you can all get stuck into this wee something I've just knocked up. Now,' she said, waving a greasy finger, 'we're going to get dressed so mind and leave some for us.'

Rosie and Burns exchanged glances. Thank goodness their friends lived near them and had seen their secret signal Burns had managed to send before their parents arrived on the scene. Ever since a very expensive 'phone bill had dropped through the letterbox they'd had to think of another way of communication.

'Grown-ups are so---o---unfair. Ma's never off the bloomin' phone,' Rosie had complained, 'but here's an idea. Let's hang a towel out of one of our windows. Then Midge and Andy'll know if we need to see them quick.'

And this was one alright. It had been one of her better ideas, Burns conceded, and made good use of the fact that, even if their friends lived practically opposite them, the busy road separating them made communication difficult. So, whilst Rosie was taking Brose inside, he'd managed to get over his recent window phobia and hang out his Batman towel. It must've worked for here they were.

"Troubles shared are troubles halved," was one of their parents' favourite sayings and just seeing Midge and Andy here made life look better. Then too, there was Midge's appetite.

Some stomachs might have heaved at the prospect of Ma's bakes, but Midge's wasn't so fussy. Midge was actually Marjory but when she was little and getting where she wasn't wanted, her parents said she was a wee pest; like a midgie.

The name stuck even if she was, like Rosie, ten years old, but much taller, thin, and always hungry.

In the absence of food she usually chewed the end of her long blonde plait. Burns thought she'd probably sucked out a colour which once might have matched her brown eyes. They sparkled as soon as she saw the bannocks. Tossing her pigtail back, she kept dropping her hand over them.

'Guess what….' Burns began, and by the time the story was finished, so were the buns.

Seeing Brose showing 'good-dog' position by sitting hard, with her eyes despondently fixed on the empty plate, Andy searched his pocket.

'Here's a wee something for a brave doggie,' he said and offered her a gob stopper. Attracted by the smell of a thousand sweeties, she licked it daintily and with increasing enthusiasm.

When it changed colour Andy gently removed it. 'My turn now,' he said as he popped it into his mouth.

Although he looked a bit like Midge, he was smaller and didn't have her appetite. He preferred sweets, especially where Ma McRae's food was concerned. The thought of it made him crunch hard on his share of the gob stopper as he said, 'But what was Picker doing with the paper anyway. Sure he's not old enough to be allowed on a paper round?'

'I dunno. He said something about a favour.' Burns's eyes were huge. He was anxious, scrubbing the freckles on his nose so hard Andy was surprised they didn't rub off.

'I bet pushing the usual boy off his bike and grabbing the papers would be his idea of a good turn. Still, I bet he's not boasting he's got a bruise, and right on his leg too,' said Rosie, and did a cartwheel to steady her nerves.

'Now Little Miss Upside-Down.' Da was back, fully dressed and eyeing the empty plate with relief. 'Get your clothes on and go down the town, buy another Inverspurtle and when you're in the paper shop, see if you can find out about The Macsnott. Nobody in their right mind should employ him. Hurry now! Your pals look ready for action.' He glanced out the window. 'And it's a bonny day for getting out too.'

Burns cheered up a bit. At least Da wasn't mad about his paper and

Rosie seemed to fancy being a real life detective more than the metal detector one she and Midge had earlier planned. She was dressed and ready in seconds.

Clutching a used envelope and pink pencil, her bum waggled busily as she made for the door, 'Come on, Midge. Let's go.'

Burns watched as her red clip-clops moved in a blur keeping up with Midge's easy lope. As soon as they were gone, he said, 'If you keep Brose company, Andy, I'll get the metal detector for us.'

He left his friend sharing his gob stopper, whilst he went to get ready. He felt faint at the thought of Picker's threat, but as time went by and he was still alive, he began to relax. He was fairly sure Macsnott actually needed his gang to operate.

They weren't usually around at weekends since they could find more places to hide from his vicious ways of enrolment than there were in the playground. And Monday was a whole two days away and with all this drama around, maybe his parents might forget about dancing.

Dressed in his Super-man top, red jogging bottoms, and green shoes with socks in stripes bright enough to cheer up anybody, Burns felt better. The sun was beginning to fight its way through the clouds. Summer was round the corner and holidays weren't far away. If he and Andy got some action with the metal detector they might even find treasure. And then they'd safely get off to Disneyland...for ever.

As always, he ignored the, 'KEEP OUT, BURNS,' sign on Rosie's bedroom door. Nipping into her room, he tore another wee strip off the wallpaper by way of signature and scouted under her bed.

'Ha! So she did pinch my batteries. No wonder my sword wasn't working.' A fluff covered spoon coloured in the pink of dead yoghurt had made a joint appearance with the metal detector. The machine bleeped.

'Greatie, greatie! It's working. Now, we're in business.' He ran downstairs.

'Come on, Andy, let's go. I feel an adventure coming on.'

8: TREASURE HUNTERS

THE McRAES lived at the bottom of Cloven Hill which overlooked the town. With its gentle contours and leafy mantle of trees it was like a sleeping green giant guarding Inverspurtle. It made its folk feel safe to wander the wooded paths leading to the top. The hill looked lovely but it had a dark past.

There was a tower at the top. It was called Kate's Keep and long ago, women thought to be witches, were hurled from there to certain death in spiked barrels. Far below, a stone marked the spot where the last one, Kate, had met her agonising end.

'Sure it wasn't a very nice way to go,' said Andy as they scrambled over the back wall between the house and the hill.

Not even Burns's imagination could cope with the idea. He shook his head. 'Mind,' continued Andy, 'my Dad says he thinks there could be treasure at Kate's Keep and at least we'd be out of his range.' He nodded at the metal detector. 'Member the rage he was in when we tried it out in our garden? He took a right feejee.'

Burns remembered Mr Macduff dancing up and down. It was an even worse sight than his parents waltzing.

'Yeh! You'd have thought he'd have been glad of someone turning the earth over.' He continued in an injured tone, 'And the worms would have liked seeing a bit of daylight an' all.'

'Aye - well - it's more than Da was. He said we'd ruined his perfect lawn. He even threw away that old horse shoe we found.' Andy sighed. 'It could have been valuable.'

The boys had taken a hand fork to help with their treasure search. As well as having its points jabbing into him through his trouser pocket, Burns was having a job keeping up with his pal. He was really fit…and he was even carrying the detector. Maybe, thought Burns, if we'd a garden as big as his with all its trees, I could build good muscles climbing them. Andy flew up trees all the time. No wonder Ma McRae called him a little monkey.

Stopping to let Burns catch up Andy said, 'Imagine building something to mark someone's horrible end. Have you ever been inside the tower?'

Burns, now completely out of puff, could only nod. He remembered going with his father.

He took the hand fork out and pretended to check the points for a sharpness, he already knew, but really to get his breath back. At length he said, 'We only got as far as the shrunken heads and man-trap display on the second floor. Da said, "We'll not bother with the view. The steps to the top are too narrow for safety."'

He knew, but didn't say, that this was really because his dad didn't have a head for heights. Every time Burns went higher than a molehill his father would shout, 'Careful!' making Burns fall in fright. Look at the accident he had flying off the wee table at home! That wasn't his fault. Adults could be a pest. It was a pity you needed one to get into the tower.

'There's three other lots of stairs and at the top you can go outside and get a good view. Still, you saw the best bits.' Andy was consoling. 'Ma took me an' Midge one day we were really bored but Midge got hungry,' he made a face, 'so we'd to leg it back home.'

At last, the boys came to the tower. It was hexagonally shaped. There were mesh covered windows higher up but the ones at ground level had been filled in. They had a blind look with arches which matched the one over the front door. It was painted a soft shade of green but the studs embedded in it made it look as if a siege was expected.

Ghost-believers figured the spirit of Kate, still haunted the hill. In such surroundings and on a wild night, you could easily imagine hearing the cries and groans of somebody in agony. Of course it might only be the wind moaning through branches of the crowding, surrounding trees.

In today's sunshine Burns was more concerned he'd get sunstroke. Andy was lucky not having his red hair or a pale skin which went bright red and had freckles like brown measles spreading across it. If they all joined up, Burns worried, how would he know if he'd caught the illness. He put his hand to his forehead. Phew! It felt alright – for the moment anyway.

Remembering the cat, he took a quick look around and began to wonder if he had actually seen it. He was glad he hadn't mentioned it to anybody. He bet they'd just have said he was making it up. It was more likely that he'd had a nightmare. It could be, thought Burns, they'd have been right.

Andy interrupted his thoughts. 'Come on, let's get started. Why don't we try where the picnic tables were last year? Sometimes folk drop money there by mistake.' He swung the machine with its long handle and saucer-like disc in a casual circle. Burns stood ready with the hand fork.

A robin hopped down from one of the tower's grilled windows to get a better view, then flew away in alarm when the detector let out a high pitched bleep.

'That was quick!' Burns rushed forward and stuck the fork into the ground. He tried to prise off the covering turf but all he managed was to cut a few blades of grass.

'Mind,' cautioned Andy, 'we don't want to get into trouble with the hill warden.'

'You mean Big George Muldoon?' Burns stopped for a moment, thinking about the unreasonableness of adults. He screwed up his face in anxiety. 'They say he thinks the Hill belongs to him an' he's awful fierce too.'

Andy felt in his pocket and handed over a Swiss knife. 'Well he's not likely to be around this early but better use this. See, Burns, the trick is to dig after you cut out a square of turf. Then you can replace it so nobody knows you've been digging. Well,' he sighed, as if remembering an unhappy episode, 'That's what my Dad said after the lawn row.'

'Right.' Burns, frowning in concentration, followed Andy's advice whilst the machine continued to bleep.

'Ach! It's only the metal of the hand fork setting it off. It's too near the machine. Look!' Andy, pointed to where Burns had thrown it aside, but a second later, the boys glimpsed something solid.

'Wait a minute!' Burns plunged one hand into the earth, then started to scrape away with both. The machine was going mental. Something black and moving near the tree caught his eye but he was too busy to lift his eyes from the ground.

Forgetting about everything else, he thought he'd explode with excitement for there, half-hidden in the disturbed earth, must surely be treasure. 🕷

33

9: MORAG OG

WHILST ANDY AND BURNS were busy on the hill, Rosie and Midge were heading towards Morag Og's house. The Og's were neighbours and young Morag was delighted that, unlike Burns's sabre, her swords didn't need batteries. She could think of loads of better uses for them than some daft dance over them. When she was expelled from highland dancing lessons, it was no hardship to the lively nine year old.

Pondering on the swords' defence potential, she swung on the Og garden gate. It helped her to think and when that got boring, she'd another ploy.

If anyone came her way, she'd quickly duck out of sight behind a nearby hedge then shout in a squeaky voice, 'What's that smell?'

It was a great game especially when it startled people and made their noses twitch. Some even shook their heads and said, 'I need to get home for a bath,' before rushing away.

But it was still early and she hadn't managed to offend anybody – yet – so, when she saw Midge and Rosie, her heart leapt. They were her friends and deserved special treatment.

She jumped off the gate and, scooping up some earth, nipped to her usual hiding place. The girls were deep in chat as they passed. If they hadn't stopped to argue about who should carry the pencil they'd have escaped the shower of earth.

'Oh hello, Morag,' said Rosie without bothering to look. 'I thought you were supposed to be highland dancing.'

Morag looked over the top of the hedge, her face as cheerfully rosy as a rising sun. It had taken her ages melting a whole bag of sugar in a bucketful of water to make the syrup she'd used to stiffen her hair. Now she was pleased that she'd something looking like a lavatory brush sitting on top of her head.

'Gavin Mactrip didn't like me slitting his trews with my swords, even tho' he was complaining he couldn't bend down,' Morag explained. 'He went and told his Mam he'd been attacked! Honestly! That's what I got for being helpful and, you know this?' She shook her head in amazement. She went and complained to the dancing teacher. Morag spread out her filthy little hands in exasperation. 'Honestly! She took a right feejee.'

'Bet it wasn't as bad as the row at our house.' Rosie shuddered and retold the story.

'Poor poor Brose,' said Morag, then hopefully, asked, 'Was Picker bleeding?'

Rosie dimpled. The sun caught on her hair and made her curls shine.

'He should have a bruise. Mind, it'll not be bad enough to keep him off school. Anyhow, I bet he wants to get even with Burns - probably flatten him. Likely it'll be first thing on Monday.' She said it in a careless way.

'An' what about you, Rosie. Are you not scared he goes for you as well?' Morag's blue eyes shone at the prospect of a Cassowary kick appearing in the playground. Being a spectator at one of Rosie's rages was worth the bore of going to school.

Midge wrinkled her nose in contempt and from her great height, looked down at her companions. 'He's too big a coward to try. Picker only picks on wee ones.'

The Og's gate needed as much oil as the McRae's one. Oblivious to its awful squeak, Morag climbed back to swing on it and said, 'We'll need to watch out for Burns.' She tapped her hair-spikes and creased her brow to show she was thinking hard.

Older by a year, she'd always looked out for him at Playschool and even though that was ages ago she still took a kindly interest in his welfare.

'Picker's really much bigger than him. Mind, the funny thing about him is that he's in the school choir. You wouldn't think he'd know a good note from a bad one.' As if to show she did, she swung the gate hard making its hinges squeal as if in agony.

Unable to stand the racket any longer, Midge linked arms with Rosie. 'C'mon - we'll need to get that paper, and if we find out anything, Morag, we'll let you know.'

And it wasn't long before they did. 🐝

10: DETECTIVE WORK

'D'YOU THINK WE SHOULD HAVE TOLD the paper shop man that Picker wasn't Hamish?' Midge asked as they sauntered home. Her long fingers searched the bottom of the crisp bag she'd recently bought. Rosie hadn't started hers. She was struggling to open the accompanying blue salt bag and having the Inverspurtle paper under her arm didn't help.

'Not just yet, Midge. If it's the Hamish I'm thinking of, that's Picker's cousin and he's nice. Always pats Brose and looks happy. We don't want to get him into trouble.'

'Is he bigger than Picker?' Midge started to jot down some notes on the envelope.

'Yes – put down much bigger.' Rosie checked Midge's spelling, 'and write that Mr Caird, the paper man, can't see a bloomin' thing without his specs. Remember him saying he took them off to rub his eyes?'

'Aye. An' he said the paper boy arrived at the same time as he laid the specs on the counter and the next thing he knew, they were on the floor and smashed. He was mad as anything and said the boy never even apologised. Och! I'm running out of space.' Midge, tiring of writing and hearing Rosie rustling her crisp bag, sighed. 'Could you not eat so near my ear?'

Rosie grinned and handed her the bag. 'Oh go on. You don't mind too much salt. I should have bought sweeties and eaten them before Andy got his hands on them.'

Nearing Morag's house, they heard voices, then saw two old ladies coming towards them and arguing.

'I never said anything about a smell,' said one, frowning as she hurried after the other.

'Well! Neither did I but I certainly heard somebody say, "what's that smell?"'

'And so did I,' replied her companion, stopping for a moment to bang her stick on the pavement, 'but I'm surprised you even thought I could be so rude.'

'Who else could it be then?'

They glanced around then, noticing Midge and Rosie, looked embarrassed and dropped their argument until the girls had passed. Once they thought they were out of earshot, they started off again.

Midge laughed, 'I'd be surprised if they didn't come to blows. Wonder what started that up.'

Rosie pointed to the Og garden gate. 'We don't need to be a detective to work that one out.'

'Tee hee!' The sound came from behind the hedge.

Midge shot behind it and pounced on the culprit. 'Morag – you wee rascal,' she cried. 'You've really upset those wifies. I think you might've even started a war between the two of them.'

Morag shook off Midge.

'Result!' she crowed, and slapped her thigh in merriment.

'What have they ever done to you?' Rosie asked in bewilderment. Sometimes she thought Morag Og was a bit too mischievous.

'One of them knocked my brother off his bike.'

'What was he doing?'

'Cycling in the park,' said Morag with a dangerous glint in her eye.

Rosie didn't much care for Morag's brother and thought that in the absence of a Cassowary, a quick whack would do him no harm. Still, she didn't want to fall out with Morag. Not only was she a little rascal but a clever one too.

Midge had more urgent matters to consider. 'My tummy's rumbling,' she said. 'It says it needs feeding. Let's go home.' She began to gnaw her plait.

'Didn't you find out anything?' asked Morag, disappointed that they were leaving. 'You promised you'd tell me.'

Rosie gave her their store-detective tale. A steady flow of traffic had begun to whistle past them so that by the end of their tale, she'd to shout over the noise.

'Don't make such a racket,' said Morag covering her ears, 'it's noisy enough as it is. You wouldn't think there was a speed limit on this road.' She grubbed around in her jeans' pocket and fished out a chewing gum wrapper.

'I'll write on this. It'll make good 'teccy stuff,' she said. She put out a hand and twiddled her fingers, 'So you'll have finished with your pencil, right?'

'Why?'

'I'm going to take down car numbers. If drivers see me doing that, it'll give them a right fright.'

The girls left Morag loving her newest way to annoy people, then, reaching the McRae gate, were surprised when grim faced Andy and Burns ran to meet them.

'Don't go inside,' Burns, looked over his shoulder, 'we don't want anyone hearing us an' guess what....' He drew his finger over his throat. 'We're in terrible trouble.

THE FRIENDS clustered in an anxious huddle at the bottom of the garden. Burns had to clamp his teeth together to stop them chattering but at last he began, 'See - we were sure we'd found treasure. We were so excited. The detector was going mental. It was buzzin' an' bleepin' all over the place, going bananas but at the end of all that, it was,' he sighed, his shoulders slumped, 'only a wee scrap of silver paper.'

Andy put in, 'It was really really disappointing - and as well as that, we were getting hungry and thirsty and we'd run out of sweets.'

'So a real crisis then?' said Midge, beginning to lose interest.

Andy nodded. 'Yeh. We thought we should just go home but then Burns said we should try under the rowan tree.'

'Uh hu, I knew it was that,' said Burns. 'I asked Da what was that scabby looking tree standing on its own and he said that's a rowan tree and they're meant to keep away evil. Da even laughed, saying that this one must be very old and from Kate's time and a sign from her proving she wasn't a witch.' He rolled his eyes and heaved a sigh. 'Some joke!'

He was about to mention the mysterious big black cat that he'd seen earlier on but Brose, tail jaunty, distracted him as, she trotted down to join them.

'Glad you're feeling better,' said Burns, fondling her ears, 'at least that's something good, eh girl?'

'Oh get on with it, Burns,' said Rosie, sighing in exasperation, 'what happened next?'

'Well, we weren't too fussed about looking but then the machine went daft – really daft this time. We got so excited!' Burns stopped a moment to consider his leg, scratch it gently, before continuing. 'We'd made a really good job of cutting out a square of grass the first time, but the second time, the ground was softer.' He sucked his lip. 'I just stuck in the hand fork and — guess what...'

'Burns!'

Andy burst in, 'We started to really dig. We were like terriers, sorry, Brose. I know you're a great digger too.'

Watching Brose wag her tail Midge said, 'Och, Andy – she knows that. Get on with it.'

'Well – just as we saw something like a tin and square shaped, Big George, yon nasty hill warden came out from behind some bushes like he was rocket-propelled. And you should've seen his face,' Andy's eyes went round as Maltesers, 'it was like a beetroot. I thought his eyes were about to pop out. Then he started to shout horrible things as well as saying we were vandals an' he was sick of people damaging his trees.'

'His trees,' said Burns with a hollow laugh. 'We hadn't touched any of the bloomin' things but I bet he reckons the ground's his too. He said that now he'd caught two people actually red handed, he'd make us pay for everybody else.' Burns's lip quivered. 'An' he'd make an example of us. An' tell our parents'n all.'

Picking up on his distress, Brose whined and gave him her paw. Midge was less sympathetic. 'You didn't give him your real names did you?'

That hadn't occurred to either boy. Girls! thought Burns, they always believed they were so smart. He wondered how they'd have coped with a spluttering fat man who only started to look less like murdering them after he pulled out an official looking notebook.

'Right!' he'd said, jotting down their details, 'I'll be round to visit your parents. I'll be telling them you were trying to kill off the only rowan tree growing on Cloven Hill and……. take that thing away.'

'It's a metal detector,' Burns had tried, hoping that Big George's well aimed kick hadn't damaged the machine. 'I don't care what it is,' Big George had bawled, 'gettit out of here.'

Now, Rosie was giving her brother a hundred per cent attention. 'So the box thing's still there?'

'Yeh – Big George never gave us a chance to tell him about it. Anyway there was no chance he'd listen. He made us put back the earth so it's all covered up again. And Big George said he never wanted to see us again.' Andy blinked hard, 'And we sure don't want to see him either.' As a sign of a caring nature, Midge tickled Andy's face with the end of her pigtail. 'I'm right glad I wasn't there and you two'll just have to pray he's got rid of his rage and forgets all about you.' She sucked her pigtail thoughtfully. 'Now we need to think up a way to get that box. After we've had some food, let's have a planning meeting in the hut.' 'Fat lot that'll do,' said Burns, already composing a dying speech in his head.

12: ESCAPE

WHEN BURNS WENT BACK INTO THE HOUSE, he wondered if dropping a clock would stop time.

'With my luck,' he gloomed, 'I'd prob'ly fast forward it. Anyway, Old Big George's bound to appear sometime an' if that's not enough there's Picker.'

The prospect of Picker Macsnot exacting revenge at school was putting him off his dinner.

'Are you all right?' his mother asked. 'You usually like stovies.' She pointed to a mixture of potatoes with meat bits sticking out of it. Abandoned, in the middle of his plate, his food resembled a hedgehog and judging by the smell of it, Burns thought, a long time dead.

'He's fine,' said Rosie, 'but you know he's not much of a meatetarian.' She kicked her brother under the table and mouthed, 'Act Normal.'

As if he could! He'd have kicked her back but, without his trainers, there wasn't much point. That's what I get for being considerate and leaving my mucky shoes outside, he thought.

'I went to a lot of bother making that meal and if you're not going to eat anymore,' said Ma, picking up her bagpipes, 'you can jolly well sort out the kitchen.'

'Aw, Ma!'

A blast of some terrible pibroch-drone drowned out further protest. Their own muttering as they struggled through a mountain of dirty dishes went unheard.

'It's so-o- unfair,' said Rosie and flicked soapy froth at Burns. Unfortunately his mouth was open at the time whilst Rosie's sympathy was underwhelming. 'Ha ha - look at you - you're foaming at the mouth.'

Enough was enough.

'Ruggabug and, You! ...To the death!' spluttered Burns. He seized Ma's fish slice and advanced, swishing and swatting ready to perfect the complete and longed for wipe-out of his sister.

'I'm telling on you.' Realising her brother had finally lost it and her cassowary leg was best used to escape, Rosie made for the door, screaming.

'Ma! Burns's swearing and he says he's gonna kill me as well.'

The bagpipes gave a dying moan. It sounded bad. There was a worrying silence then, proving it had been used for Ma to fill her lungs, came a yell, 'Is there no peace for anybody around here? You Two…Out… Now!'

Burns rushed outside only to discover that his trainers had gone. He hopped about desperately searching for them.

He'd reached the rubbish bins at the back of the house when he heard the doorbell ring. As if he hadn't enough to contend with! What if it was Big George Muldoon? He had to move but where were his bloomin' trainers?

Proudly bearing one, Brose emerged from behind the rubbish bins. She looked very pleased with herself. The shoe dangled from a toothy grin. She didn't usually smile like that and he hadn't noticed her teeth before. Today they looked huge and somehow familiar. But not in Brose. People did say dogs grew to look like humans. She must be growing to look like one and someone he knew rather well.

Rosie started to laugh. 'Oh no! '

Da McRae's voice came echoing down the garden, 'Hath anybothy theen my teeff?'

'Here. Take these. Quick!' Rosie, behind him, was dancing with impatience.

Burns, appalled, looked at the pink furry slippers she was thrusting at him.

'I'm not putting these on. You wouldn't even wear them.'

'They're gross and too small for me but you've no choice. Come on, Burns. We need to go. Da'll blame us and murder Brose if he finds her wearing his teeth.'

It was as tricky getting them back as it was the trainer but Rosie eventually managed. 'I hope Da knows to wash them,' she said, putting the teeth on top of one of the bins. Then, as she knelt down to pat Brose, she crooned, 'You are a bad dog! Go inside and hide with My Little Ponies now!'

'Where did you put my other shoe?' whispered Burns, but Brose, deprived of her chew mate didn't reply. Instead she slunk away.

Rosie was full of admiration. 'See? She knows where she'll be safe.

Now, hurry.'

'Burnth!' His father's voice came from the front door. 'There are you?'
He sounded odd.

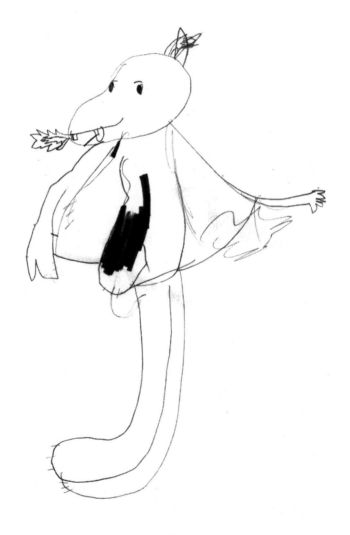

13: AN IMPORTANT MEETING

DA MACSPORRAN must have got fed up of looking for Burns and whoever had called at the house had been invited in. The children crept away hoping, that if it was Big George, he'd been struck dumb. Seeing Da without his teeth often had that effect.

They managed to sneak un-noticed to the Macduff garden until Andy sentinel - posted up a Douglas fir tree, spied them. Loyal as he was to Burns, he couldn't help chuckling when he saw the pink slippers.

'Stylish eh?' he said, firing down a fir cone.

'Don't you start,' shouted Burns. He mopped his brow and wondered how girls could be bothered wearing things which, at the same time as slowing you down, made your feet sweat. With his extra toe especially protesting, he shuffled towards the hut which had once been the Macduff's garden shed.

Midge artwork of skull and crossbones was newly painted on its red door. It showed a change of ownership but remnants of an old life remained. A hand powered lawnmower that Mr Macduff had thought an essential buy until he'd had to push it, now lay unused against a wall.

A rat lived behind it. Today, its long tail coiling out from the mower showed he was at home. Fazed neither by the Keep Out signs nor the skull and cross bones, he was responsible for the gnawed hole at the bottom of the door.

The children had good reason to be grateful to him. Mrs Macduff had taken one look at the hole and declared that a new electric mower needed a new rat tooth-proof house where flexes and such would be safe. Now a posh replacement with granite-harled walls stood nearer the house leaving the old hut spare and for the children's use.

It was just big enough to hold them and the old mower, as well as a bag of potatoes. This had been left because the Macduffs didn't fancy eating them when it was obvious Rat had had the first bite. Behind the mower, he tidied his whiskers, watching as the children piled in, keeping the door open for more space.

'See he's keeping his tail out 'cos Brose's not about,' said Andy. 'If she was, she'd be trying to pull it.'

'She hasn't much of one herself. Maybe she wants his one.' Rosie laughed, then, prodding Midge's arm painted black, she said, 'I see you've had time to do some more artwork. Mmmm. I like it. Any more paint?' Already she was pulling up her jersey sleeve and twiddling her fingers as if she couldn't wait to get started. 'If we all painted ourselves we could be the Black Hand Gang.'

Burns picked his nose. 'Count me out.' He removed a potato which had escaped from the bag. It had made the floor even more uncomfortable to sit on. 'An' I dunno why you're all so cheerful. It's been a terrible morning. I don't know how many times I thought I was a goner. '

'Och, Burns - you're such a gloom. We just need to prove Big George wrong.' Midge wriggled with impatience, 'and that's,' she waved a finger at the end of each letter as she spelt it out, 'SIMPUL!'

'How?' Andy sounded unsure. 'We can't just leave the box. It could be the find of the year. 'Burns and I've been dying to find treasure and a glimpse of a box and this,' he waved the silver sweetie paper in the air, 'is the nearest we've ever got to something big.'

'You haven't something else in your pocket you could share?' Midge asked hopefully, but Andy ignored her. He was looking at Burns but he was worrying his finger nails so he continued, 'I certainly don't want to be caught by Big George Muldoon again. I think he'd exterminate us if he could.'

'Then there's only one thing we can do.' Midge stood up. She looked at the group, stood tall, drew breath, then said, 'We'll just have to go and look when it's dark and nobody's around.'

A hush fell. In silence, each youngster considered Midge's idea. They were torn between fear of the unknown and excitement of the challenge. Cloven Hill in daytime was one thing, but to go there at night and in the dark, was something else.

Quietly, as if giving them a trial run, the door closed. They were left in a suffocating black space. Then, as they sat, frozen with fear and blinded, there was a deafening bang. ❧

14: A NEW MEMBER

A SECOND BANG was followed by a third then another. The noise, made worse by the hut's corrugated iron roof, was deafening. Then it stopped. Silence. All that Burns could hear was his heart thumping and the sound of everybody breathing quickly. Just as they became aware of the heavy smell of old grass left on the mower's blades, they heard a muffled giggle.

Midge rose. She pushed open the door and yelled, 'Morag Og – You wee…!'

'Ha Ha. Got a fright did you?' Morag, doubled over, was holding onto a branch three times her size.

'Cowardy, cowardy, custards!' She wiped away tears of laughter with the back of a hand as black as Midge's recently painted one. 'I got you lot this time.'

'And I'll get you, Morag Og!' Burns, galvanised into action, raced to the door. He'd picked up the potato. Now he hurled it at her. Ducking, Morag shouted, 'Missed!' and watched as it hit a tree. There was a splatting sound like an egg breaking.

'Hmm!' Midge had followed its flight with a thoughtful eye. 'Let's see.' She spilt a few potatoes out of the bag into her hand, tested one's weight, then took aim.

Morag ran round the hut with a screech of half alarm, half laughter, but Midge, ignored her and was out of the shed and facing the tree.

'Aye. Another bull's eye,' she cried as her potato splattered to its end.

'Hey! This looks like a really cool game!' said Rosie and rolled up her sleeves.

'Yeh. Splatty the tattie,' chanted Morag. 'Why haven't we thought this one up before?'

'We'll need to leave some for Rat,' worried Burns, 'it must be terrible to starve to death.' He slipped a few potatoes behind the lawn mower, then dragged the bag to the door.

Midge watching the rat tidying his tail out of the way said, 'Look, he's maybe making more room for his share. How sensible's that?'

'Very,' Rosie was sarcastic, 'and I s'pose if he could count he could take a score too. ' She turned to Andy. 'But you always know how many orange Smarties there's in a tube. And you're good at counting so you do it.'

Ok.' Andy checked his fingers as if making sure he'd still got ten. He nodded to Burns. 'You go first, but…' he looked round the group, 'are the points for aim or sound?'

Midge nodded towards the new garage with its harled walls. 'Both. But I think that'd be better than the tree. See…' As if bowling for cricket, she threw her potato.

Like it was bent on its own destruction it flew towards the wall smashing into it, in an explosion of tattie bits.

'Brill!' shouted Morag.

'Wait!' said Andy, 'it's not your turn.'

But inspired by Midge's targeting skills, and taking a handful of potatoes, she had worked herself into a frenzy. The wall, apparently presenting itself as hostile territory, got a fusillade of potatoes.

'Come on, Troops,' Morag screamed, beckoning with her free hand, 'let's end our deadly foe!'

'Ok, lads, what are we waiting for?' Rosie positioning herself behind Morag soon got into the swing of things.

Andy and Burns looked at each other, shrugged, then joined in.

'Mortar fire!' yelled Andy. 'Go for it, Burns.'

Burns had to admit that it was exciting seeing the wall disappear under tattie garnish.

'There's quite a pattern in there,' Midge, put her head sideways, 'if we all aim to the right, we could make a wall mural. It's already a bit like the Loch Ness monster.'

'Yeh - and it could come alive and eat Picker,' Rosie's eyes gleamed and she nudged Burns who'd managed for a few blissful moments to forget all about him.

'Aw, Rosie - give me a break,' Burns said in the moany way that always set Rosie's teeth on edge. Then he returned to the task in hand, loving the way he could practise destruction even if it only was on a potato. Splat!

Burns blinked. For a second he thought he might have glimpsed a black cat–like shadow, but he forgot because this really was a great game.

It totally engrossed everybody until a cry rang out. 'And what is the meaning of this?'

Un-noticed by the children, Mr Macduff, Mr McRae and Big George Muldoon had appeared. They stood in a half circle; each looking more furious with every gathering moment. 🍂

15: A TERRIBLE ROW

J<small>UST LIKE THE TATTIES</small> which had disintegrated on the garage wall it looked as if each adult was about to explode. But this time on the spot and into a mass of red blotchy bits.

Mr Macduff had shouted first. Now he was speechless and apart from his Adam's apple jumping up and down, motionless.

Mr McRae, however, could move. And now, in fact, he was dancing. Not the waltz which Burns would actually have welcomed but jigging up and down in fury. Not only had Big George Muldoon interrupted his snooze in front of the telly, but his teeth were still lost. It made shouting difficult, but he persevered. 'I can'th believe I'm theeing thith,' he cried. 'Your bonny thed, Hecthor!'

As if he hadn't enough to contend with! His friend and neighbour's much prized new shed looked as if it had a dose of chickenpox. Much as he hated to admit it, it was plain that all the kids were involved in making this mess: had they not just been caught in the act?

Now he was beginning to believe that not only the boys, but the girls, were the hooligans Big George hinted they were.

The warden had arrived at their house.

'Without so much as a "good morning" he'd pounded on the door and shouted, 'McRae?' Having answered it and, because of the lack of teeth, Mr McRae nodded. He was immediately sorry that he had because, Big George, finger stabbing and shouting, launched off.

'I've just stopped your lad and his pal destroying Cloven Hill. D'you know this?' Big George had stopped to fill his lungs, then he was off again. 'Your son and his friend were digging up the place. They were going at it like mad things.'

'Thurely not,' Mr McRae tried.

'Yeth.' Big George's face went as red as his braces as he corrected himself. He hurried on. 'I actually caught them right in the act. Now, I'm sorry to say this, but it's plain to me, those boys have no sense of discipline or respect. In my humble opinion,' here Big George looked as if it was anything but, he pulled on his braces, before continuing, 'boys like them should be locked up for a week if not more. They're a pair of hooligans. Hooooo-leee-guns!' He seemed to like the word because he was about to say it again when Mr McRae held up his hands. He was usually in charge of shouting and didn't appreciate competition.

'Whoa!'

Had he been in full possession of his teeth he might have put up a better defence. Instead he'd settled for inviting Big George into the house thinking that the whole matter of metal detectors and naughty children could be discussed in a reasonable - even cosy manner.

He planned on offering and soothing his guest with a glass of Macdrouth's Heather Cordial. He knew Mrs McRae wouldn't approve but was confident she was safely out of the way.

He reckoned that after a drink or two, the boys could be found, apologies nicely delivered and nicely accepted. Then he could get back to the important things in life.

Once he'd got Big George inside, he said, 'They're good kids really,' to which Big George had responded with the same, 'Really?' but in quite a different way.

And then he heard Mrs McRae. By the sound of the heavy thumping from upstairs, she must be weight lifting. She could easily add to her husband's troubles. If she saw the cordial, she might confiscate it. Then she might produce the usual vile tea and the week-old bannocks lying in the bottom of the bread bin. He'd seen them two days ago and even then, they wore a mantle of green mould.

'Natural penicillin!' he'd guarantee she'd say.

'Just the thing to finish off our guest,' he'd have wanted to reply - witty as you like, but, reluctant to add a corpse to his problems, he decided to relocate Big George.

'Come on,' he said, 'I know where we'll get the boys but mind the road.'

Even if a JCB had been coming towards him, Big George was oblivious to all but getting those bally kids sorted out. He'd been brushing up on metal detector rules and this was the perfect opportunity to give a lecture on them. Not only had he found the boys in a fresh bout of vandalism but he was witnessing it in a garden where there were other brats as well and with the fathers present.

This was a captive audience, even if they were freaky. The Macduff girl was easily recognisable because she looked so like her brother, but what was she doing with a black arm? Then, Big George thought, there was the McRae guy. He hadn't teeth and his son was now wearing pink slippers. Big George consulted his watch. And all at this time in the afternoon! So he wasn't dreaming.

Odder and odder, mused Big George, having another pull on his bright red braces. Still, he had a message and he was on a mission to deliver it. 'What people and their unruly children get up to on their own property is their business,' he drilled out the well-rehearsed words, 'but digging holes in public places is a felony.'

Burns wasn't sure what that meant but it sounded painful. Anyway Big George was off again. 'And anybody using a metal detector should have asked for permission to use it on land that doesn't belong to them. And,' he wagged a finger, 'since Cloven Hill belongs to our Council I doubt very much if they'd have got it.'

This seemed to cheer him. He continued in a breezier way, 'and even if anything was found, it would belong to the local council and if it was old and of interest to Inverspurtle, they'd most likely give it to the town's museum.'

Mr Macduff had recovered his speech enough to ask, 'And if it was money?'

Big George was delighted to show off more knowledge. 'Money!' he treated himself to a scornful laugh. 'In that case, it should go to the Police Station. Mind you, there's not likely to be anything of value at Kate's Keep.' He drew breath, making the buttons of his coat strain against the tummy that gave him his name, 'but of course, there's plenty damage that can be done - especially unnecessary holes.'

'Well, thath'll not be a problem. The methal dethector's confithcated from now on,' said Da McRae. He looked at his watch, 'Now I'm thure you'll want to get back to your work, Mr Multhoon. Reth athured, you'll have no more problemth with uth or our children.'

Mr Macduff cleared his throat. Big George hoped that even if he was a little man he was getting ready to give those awful children a very big row. The thought pleased him. Then, glancing at the shed door, he suddenly noticed its permanent resident sunning itself in the doorway.

Big George hated rats. In fact was terrified of them. Not only did they too, make holes, they could run up the leg of your trousers as well.

The very thought of one gnawing his way to freedom made him reverse, whilst making a big show of looking at his watch. Continuing to step back, he said, 'You're right. I do need to get back to duties. Goodness knows I've plenty to do without having to make these sort of calls.' And then he turned and was off.

As he bobbed off, he reminded Burns of a Xmas pudding on the run, whilst Mr Macduff sticking out his neck looked like a tortoise out for an amble.

It was too much! He thought of sad things. How dead Brose looked after Picker had nearly killed her. That didn't work. He bit inside his cheek hard, and pulled his nose. That was painful but useless. He remembered the awfulness of Ma's home baking and swallowed. Still, he couldn't keep down a terrible bubble of hysteria. It was uncontrollable and dreadfully welling up and about to engulf his whole body. His shoulders heaved.

Any minute now, a giggle was going to burst out and he just knew he was going to die… laughing. 🐾

16: MORAG TO THE RESCUE

A HOT TEAR ESCAPED down Burns's face and landed on Morag's hand. Immediately she twigged. He was either going to burst or have hysterics. Idly kicking an escapee potato to help her think, she paused, then swung into action.

'Wa-aa-ah. Boo Hoo!'

Her cries stopped Mr Macduff mid breath. 'I want my Mammy, an' I wanna go home,' she bubbled. Tears spurted out in an endless spray. She continued sobbing, turning volume up to mega blast. 'I'm so-o-o- frightened by big bad men.'

On account of his size, Mr Macduff thought this didn't apply to him but Morag was even smaller than him. She sounded so disconsolate, he immediately reduced his rage to a feeble, 'I expect you all know not to do this sort of thing ever again.'

Still Morag went on bawling. The children gathered round patting her heaving shoulders. Burns, grateful his had stopped, thought Morag was brilliant – she really was! He joined in the reproachful barrier between his heroine and the dads.

'Morag never cries,' said Rosie in a shocked way and let her hand hover over the sobbing girl showing she might be too sensitive even for a kindly touch. As if to prove the point, Morag roared harder.

Mr McRae, suspecting the tables about to turn, handed Rosie a hanky and said as briskly as he could without teeth, 'Thell Morag thoo blow her noth and thop thath din.'

It was all too much! Morag's racket was giving him a sore head and his son's choice of footwear, sorer eyes. He groaned.

Picking up on this, Mr Macduff said, 'Ah well, I suppose it's not the end of the world and I hope you've all learnt your lesson. Right now, metal detectors are off limits. In the meantime, if you clean up this mess, I'm sure we'll forget all about this nonsense. Come on, Jimmy,' he turned to Mr McRae, 'What about some of your Macdrouth Cordial then I'll help you look for your teef – I mean teeth.'

The minute they were gone, Morag's blubbering stopped.

'Is that them really away?' she said, blowing her nose like the sound of an elephant trumpeting, and scrubbing her face dry. 'Jings! Your Das don't half go on.' She blinked hard, shook her head and yawned. 'Crying's hard work. I'm exhausted.'

'It certainly worked. You saved my bacon,' Burns was grateful. 'I thought I was going to explode back there.'

'How d'you manage to cry like that?' asked Andy. He'd been sure Morag would never laugh again and was worried the fathers would have to live with the disgrace of it.

'S'easy,' smirked Morag. 'I just imagine all my pet rats have died----and off I go.' She looked round the circle of children, and seeing their admiration, quickly cashed in on it. 'Anyway, why were you lot having a meeting? Is it a secret? 'Cos if it is, you can trust me. I'm good at that. I never told my teacher for a week that my Da's only got nine toes now.' It was a good way to get complete attention.

Burns thought that if it wasn't likely to be extremely painful he could maybe donate his spare one, whilst the others chorused, 'How?'

'Can't tell you. It's a secret,' said Morag and shut her mouth with the finality of a trap door closing.

Everybody knew that if it hadn't been for Morag, the dads would still be going on and on. Undoubtedly, she'd proved her worth. What was more, she was brave, and they'd need plenty courage to get them up Cloven Hill if they did go and in the middle of the night. Not only that, they'd just found out that her father only had nine toes! Give them a week and they'd find out why.

Midge looked over her shoulder. 'Right. Let's go back into the hut then we can talk in private.'

As they all squeezed into the hut, they told their new gang member about the boys' strange find and wondering when would be the best time to go back for it.

Morag's eyes shone with excitement. She said, 'Why don't we go tonight then? Else somebody else might get there before us. I could bring my swords,' she spiked her hair and looked fierce, 'and my Da's got a super torch. It's brill. Just the thing for showing us the way and finding treasure.'

'Yeh. And we could wear dark clothes and blacken our faces so nobody could see us.' Rosie was eager, hopping on one leg in excitement.

'Midge's paint would be perfect and see, she's already got one arm done. I think Morag's right. We should go tonight.'

Andy stuck out his chin. 'No chance. I've had enough excitement for one day. I don't want to go tonight —or any other night. So count me out.' He folded his arms, pouted his lips and glowered at the floor. 'It's not worth the row.'

Midge agreed. Her stomach had been rumbling for the past half hour and she was worried she'd run out of steam before getting the others to help wash down the wall. Her father had previously promised to take his family to Hamish's Happy Haggis Land for tea and she didn't know if this would still be on. A nice apology note and a clean wall might just save the day.

'Why don't we leave it till next weekend,' she suggested, getting up and opening the door, 'by that time our folk will have forgotten everything and not be watching us all the time.' She looked into the distance as if she was a fortune teller. 'If we all keep this a secret, nobody else will get to it before then.'

'Great idea.' Burns headed for the door and would've been off, had Midge not been quick to stand on the too large slippers. She held her hand up like a bobby stopping traffic.

'Woah! You're forgetting the wall. Look, let's get out the garden hose. It's good fun really and we can take shot about.'

Soon, a high speed jet of water was being directed in the general direction of the shed. When it was Morag's turn, Midge had to jump to avoid her wild aim as she told Rosie she was afraid their father might cancel their visit to Haggis Land. Tossing her well chewed pigtail over her shoulder, she added, 'and the trouble is that I don't really understand what he meant when he shouted, "what is the meaning of this?"'

'Neither did I,' Rosie shook her head in puzzlement. Then her face cleared as she said. 'I know! Why don't we just write we are all sorry for it. That should do.'

At last, with the wall returned to its original if boring state, a note was written. It was short with Midge adding some creative swirls to bulk it up. It said, Dear Mr Macduff, we are very sorry for what is the meening of this. We didn't meen any harm. Then everybody headed for home, Rosie, lightening her way in cartwheels.

'I hope our note does the trick,' said Burns his slippers glimmering pinkly in the gathering dusk, 'Andy's promised to save me a bit of black bun if they get to Haggis Land.'

'Yuck!' said Morag, 'I'd rather eat frog spawn.' She nudged him enough to make him wobble. 'Come on, Burns. I'll race you. Last one home's a hairy kipper.'

17: PICKER STRIKES

'**M**ONDAY, FUNDAY! WAKEY WAKEY. TRALAH!'
Burns groaned. His mother was a terrible singer. He buried
his head under his pillow but he could still hear her from
downstairs. How could anybody be in such a horrible bright and
cheerful mode?

Now she was shouting, 'Go on, Brose – tell him it's a lovely morning
and long past time to get up.'

Burns loved their dog but her breath was especially awful in the mornings
and now she'd powered out of Rosie's room and found him, she was
ecstatically licking his face. The smell of sewage filled the room.

'Aw, Brose! You stink!'

Oblivious to criticism, Brose wriggled in delight. On a foraging
mission, she burrowed under the bed clothes, her small body, quivering
with excitement. Burns really couldn't understand how she could be
happy just sniffing.

He'd thought he could get off school by saying he'd a sore stomach.
Now he actually did feel sick. Leaving Brose to luxuriate in his bed,
he fled to the toilet.

'Ah! You're up. Good! But why are you not dressed?' Ma checked her
watch as he staggered downstairs.

'I feel awful,' he slumped across the kitchen table. Ma stopped stirring
the pan with its grey gluey mess bubbling in it and glanced at him
for a quarter of a second. 'M'm. I must say, you're looking a bit peaky.
Still,' she returned to her cauldron, 'once you've had a nice big plate of
porridge setting you up for the day, you'll feel better. Then you can go
and put on your clothes, but you'd better hurry. Rosie's already gone.'

'I'm too ill to eat anything.'

'Nonsense.' Ma banged a plate down in front of Burns. His stomach
lurched but his mother had a look in her eye that made a stomach, no
matter how hard it lurched, change its mind and settle down to deal
with something like concrete.

Burns toyed with idea of saying how near to death he really was. As a
starter, he could maybe faint on his way out. That must surely prove

something as well as saving him from the hard work of speaking. In the past he'd found that any mention of illness triggered Ma off into a fit of hoovering. She'd broom round the house until the noise became so endless, the sufferer would get up from their sick bed just to get away from the racket.

He supposed he wasn't ill enough for his mother to notice. You wouldn't think she'd been a nurse. If you really, really couldn't move, she'd consult her old nursing book. It had some awful pictures in it. Burns and Rosie had spent hours looking at them and knew there were lots of things that could go wrong with you. Diseases were lying about just waiting to attack.

'See how much worse things could be?' was all Ma McRae would say. 'Now where did I put my thermometer?'

Actually Burns knew there wasn't a cure for terror and he'd just been told to get dressed. Glumly, he put on his school uniform, wondering how his parents would feel when he came home in bits. The thought of them weeping over his broken body sufficiently cheered him up enough to jump from the top of the stairs to the bottom. Flight was fun. It also helped make stodgy porridge go down.

He seriously considered running away. With Rosie having already gone, how'd she know? Then he considered that even if she was in the Big Ones' part of the playground which was on the other side of the school, she'd soon get to hear he'd gone missing.

Moodily heading out the door, he muttered to himself, 'S'pose she'd just go and say it proves I'm a wuss.' He hadn't been reassured when Rosie had tried to cheer him up the previous night. She'd slapped him cheerily on the back as she said, 'Och! You'll be safe enough. Picker shouldn't be in your playground anyway. He'll be on our bit.'

He thought about Andy but even if he was waiting at the gate for him, he felt as alone as a soldier going to war. He put his shoulders back, stood as tall as he could, and as he left the house, said in as loud a voice as he could manage, 'Farew-e-e-e-ll then.'

'Bye,' said Ma McRae in an absent minded way. 'Now where's that dog? She needs a bath.'

'Thanks, You Caring Person,' said Burns and slammed the door shut. Ma yanked it open. 'Here! Pop these into Morag's house,' she said, thrusting the pink slippers at Burns, 'They're too small for Rosie but they might fit Morag.'

'Morag'll never wear these. I know she won't.'

'Course she will. Now, go!'

As if he hadn't plenty to think about. Now he had those bloomin'awful slippers. He joined Andy and once they were well out of earshot, said, 'I'm gonna get rid of them. Morag's never going to wear them.'

As they neared the school, Andy pointed to a rubbish bin at the entrance, 'Hey! Why don't you could put them in there? Nobody'll be any the wiser.'

Burns brightened. 'Great idea. She'll be glad she's not got to do it herself. I think she's here already. I'm sure that's her voice.'

Andy nodded his head in the direction of their latest gang member. 'Yeh. She likes to get here early to stop anyone else from taking over.'

They watched Morag who was bossing a gang of little girls with hair in bunches and no teeth. Already they were lined up on the grass doing hand stands. Andy said in admiration, 'She's really strict. She's even worse than Midge.'

'Or Rosie,' said Burns grimly.

'Higher! Higher!' Morag leader-bellowed, her mouth as wide as a sergeant major. Apart from the felt like patch at the back of her head which her brush had missed, her hair shone like a halo. If it had been anybody other than Morag, she'd have been mistaken for an angel. When she saw the boys, she waved, then got back to yelling. 'Hup, Hup Go! Go!'

The sweet little girls huffed and puffed, their faces bright with upside down-ness.

Picker Macsnot had been busy assembling his troops too. Seeing Burns and Andy, about a dozen big boys slouched towards them.

'You're supposed to be in the Big Ones part of the playground.' Burns was surprised his voice wasn't a squeak.

'Ho! Here you talk, you'd think you were a hero,' sneered Picker. He turned to his gang. 'Right, Boys. Let's just get him now.' He punched his fist into the palm of his other hand.

Burns went from thinking Morag's gang was full of silly giggly girls to the view that it was a most attractive sight. He went to join them but his exit strategy was cut off by the boys. Surrounding him, they began to close in.

'Going somewhere, McRae?' Picker stuck his white face into Burns's. His breath, like a crate of rotten fish made Broses' seem like a fresh air round and at least she hadn't last week's mince stuck in her teeth.

Picker shot his hand out, took a fistful of Burns's hair, then jerked his head back. He hissed, 'Huh! Think you're smarter than me? And – you laughed at me. Some joke eh?' He bared his teeth – definitely last week's mince. 'Nobody – but nobody does that without paying a price. Isn't that right, Boys?'

'Aye, Picker,' came back a chorus.

Burns wasn't sure to either scream with the pain of having his head pulled back or be grateful it was marginally out of range of his enemy's halitosis.

The everyday sounds and even Morag's voice died away. A seagull perching on top of the school roof was waiting. At playtime he'd be scavenging play piece stuff dropped by the pupils. In the meantime, he passed the time stamping his feet. Maybe the daft bird thought he could attract worms to his high-up lookout.

Burns would have given anything to be there with him. Instead, and to his huge surprise, Ma's voice reached him.

'I don't know how you managed to lose a trainer. You'll just have to wear your heavy shoes today. I don't know why you don't like them. They cost a bonny penny and they're good for settling arguments.' She'd toed the air giving a fair impression of a goal scorer.

As that vision faded, it was replaced by a buzzing sound. Then Burns's foot lashed out.

'Ruggabug!'

As shoe connected with shin, Picker yelped. Had the seagull been interested, he'd have seen, far below, a boy with a tuft of hair in one hand, hopping on one foot whilst another lad, face equally white, and with a wee baldy patch, was legging it in the opposite direction.

'Gettim!' yelled Picker nursing his leg.

Some of the gang had begun to move away but reassembled quickly to cut off Burns's escape. He checked both ways but all that he could now see was a line of menacing figures closing in. They turned to Picker waiting for instructions.

Things were looking grim for Burns. Then adding to his misery, some one, somewhere shouted, 'A fight! A fight!'

It was like a call to arms. Attracted by the noise, senior pupils from the other playground area came to investigate. Sides began to form. An excited buzz swept the playground with others joining the call. 'A fight! A fight!'

Plainly Picker was furious. The sore leg made him hopping mad and his language would have made the McRae swear box explode. Spilling oaths, he limped towards Burns.

Over the tumult, Burns heard Andy cry, 'I'm telling on you, Picker.' Out of the corner of his eye, he saw his friend running towards the school doors.

Things were bad enough without this. Andy would be thinking he was doing the best thing but now everybody, in fact the whole school, would get into trouble on his account. With his luck, he'd probably be blamed for starting the fight. It was so unfair, but what could he do?

He checked his foot. At least it hadn't suffered collateral damage. There was still a good kick in there. He readied for action. 'Ruggabug,' he whispered to give himself courage. He shook his head like a boxer entering the last round.

'Come on, Picker. Let's see what you're made of...'

18: A TESTING TIME

NORMALLY, the school bell was louder than the shouty, spoon-bashing dinner-lady. It interrupted play at inconvenient times and returned the pupils to a place, many considered worse than jail. Today, however, the call to classroom, was for Burns the best sound in the world.

Picker snarled in frustration. He backed off. Bunching his fist, he limped off to the other side of the school, calling over his shoulder, 'I'll see you later, ye wee thug. See Playtime? You're gonna be for it…then.'

Burns joined his class line trudging into school. He'd been so busy trying to remember Rosie's advice on kicks, he'd forgotten to dump the slippers. Biting his lip had been painful so he chewed his cheek. That wasn't any better.

As weapons, his shoes had done better than he'd thought but he wasn't sure they'd work again. It was a pity Rosie was in the senior bit of the school. She was one of the few who hadn't come to spectate. She might have been impressed by his defensive technique, but, he thought miserably, she was probably having a good laugh with her friends about her own tackle against Picker.

Whilst Andy's solution of getting adult help could get everybody into trouble, it was frightening that amongst all the ranks of pupils who had gathered, no one had come to help him. He could have fainted with terror but falling down brought its own risks.

'Don't mess with Picker,' he recalled over-hearing. Even now he was in class, his prospects remained bleak with Miss Crowe, the class teacher looking crosser than usual with some red stuff stuck at the corner of her mouth.

Wee Bobby Dickie who sat next to Burns, put his hand to his mouth and whispered, 'Either Mrs Dracula's in town or that's raspberry jam.'

'Probly' saving it for her play piece,' Burns muttered back.

'Quiet!' Miss Crowe, stood glaring, arms crossed at her blackboard. It was covered in figures where seven, the pupils least favourite figure, monopolised.

'Ooh, No. It's times tables time! I hate them,' muttered Bobby who only smiled outside the classroom.

Unlike Bobby, Miss Crowe thought of the classroom as a home spoilt by children.

Thinking about that gave her lungs extra power as she yelled, 'Do I have to say it again? Quiet! I'll have no noise in my classroom.'

She squinted down a long nose on which black rimmed spectacles perched. She shoved back a lock of her frizzled grey hair. 'Now, as you're all aware, I'm going to retire at the end of this term. But before then, I'm determined you're all going to be able to do multiplication and that,' she rapped her desk with a chalk-covered hand making something like a dust cloud rise from it, 'means knowing your times tables.'

Bobby sneezed.

'Silence!' Miss Crowe evil-eyed round the room. 'I'm going to make quite sure everybody in this class knows how to do them,' she inflated her chest, so that it almost hid the blackboard then continued, 'so, I'm setting this test and I want a hundred per cent marks from everybody. Otherwise there'll be no playtime.'

The class sighed, feeling as trapped as something under their teacher's false teeth and apparently bothering her. She opened her desk and bent over it, pretending to be busy and giving the class a chance to exchange knowing looks.

They knew she was actually swirling her tongue under her teeth to get rid of something., they suspected was a seed from that raspberry jam caught at the side of her mouth.

They also knew she'd feel better when she surfaced because she'd a leather strap in that desk. It reminded her of the good old days when teachers were allowed to use ones on scholars to help them 'get' their tables.

'Clack!' The sound of her teeth being re-settled mixed with a Bang as she slammed the desk lid shut. 'Right!' she shouted, picking up a long wooden pointing stick, 'I'm going to get some hard work out of you. Take your jotters and write down your answers to those sums I've put on the board.'

She gave it a whack. A cloud of chalk rose in the air for a moment covering her in a fine layer of dust.

'When you've finished you'll swap with the person next to you so they can correct them when I give the answers.'

She held up the stick using it as an extension to her pointy finger. 'And there'll be no cheating because I'll be checking your books afterwards. Now…Go!'

The room was already stuffy. Miss Crowe didn't like fresh air. She leant against the radiator warming her soft plump hands. There was silence except for the occasional false teeth rattle as she stood, re-checking her gums. Whilst the class fought its way through the traps and pitfalls Miss Crowe had set in big angry looking figures written in red chalk, there was a distinct smell of rubbing out.

Wondering if it was as heavy as his heart, Burns rested his head on one hand whilst he wrote. Unfortunately for this particular day anyway, he happened to be good at sums.

'It's 'cos you've eleven toes,' Rosie, who wasn't wonderful at counting said it in an accusing way. 'They've given you practise at putting difficult numbers together.'

He'd have been quite happy to stay in at playtime but he'd enough problems without being the reason for keeping everybody else in. If he did make a mistake, people would suspect he was up to something. He blew his fringe from his eyes, then, just as Miss Crowe rapped out, 'Stop!' he shoved down the last answer.

As slowly as an elephant recovering from a sleeping dart, the class came to life. Miss Crowe rattled on, 'Right! Swap books in a clockwise direction. Quickly now.'

She could chant any times tables like a bad spell, and for each answer and as a bonus, proceeded to do so, rolling her tongue lovingly around the figures. Seven times seven appeared no less than, Burns was sure, seventy times.

He could have put enough crosses on Bobby's book to make it look like a soppy letter, but he'd given him such a pleading look, Burns hadn't the heart. Miss Crowe gave poor Bobby a hard time just because he preferred fresh air to her classroom and once, when he seemed to have difficulty breathing, told her about the benefits of an open window. She'd never forgotten it.

But now she was running out of steam. She'd come to the end of the sums. It was 10.29. A minute to go and it would be the interval.

'Hands up those who've got crosses on their work,' she said, tapping the pointer hard on the floor and looking around.

There was no response. Everybody kept their heads down.

'What! Nobody? Don't tell me you got yours right, Bobby?'

'Please Miss, yes Miss, Burns's corrected it, Miss.' Bobby looking surprised, saw that indeed he had and hoped the teacher didn't recognise Burns's spidery written corrections with big ticks smudging them.

The teacher sounded disappointed. 'Is that so, Burns? I can hardly believe it.'

The bell rang saving Burns from answering. The class gently levered themselves out from their desk, almost afraid to breathe. With a bit of luck, the old bag needed a break too. They crept out quietly, holding their crisp ones so carefully they wouldn't rustle, scared Miss Crowe might yet check their books and amazed and relieved when she didn't. Burns tagged on slowly behind, reluctant to follow.

Once outside, the class broke free. He heard them running, shouting and playing 'catchies' with their crisp bags. He liked people having fun but now the others' high spirits left him feeling scared and alone. He needed a friend but Andy must have slipped out before him.

Trudging towards the school entrance, he saw him. He was waving and pointing and crying, 'Watch out!'

But he was too late. Picker had been hiding behind the door. As he pounced, he snaked a skinny arm round Burns's throat who just managed, 'Gettoff!' before he was dragged into the nearby boys' toilet.

The last thing he saw before the door was slammed behind them and Picker's gang emerged from the cubicles, like creatures of the sewer, was Andy's face. It looked as if it'd been melted. 🐛

19: A TERRIBLE ENCOUNTER

Fear lent power to Burns's feet. He lashed out.

'O-o-oh!' Squealed a gang member, 'Hey, Picker, you never said he was sae vicious.'

For a glorious moment, Burns felt in control. Left, right, up and down went his feet, making contact every time. Joining in, and as effective, his elbows jabbed: sharp: mean.

'Ouch! That's sair.'

Result!

Keeping clear of damage, Picker yelled, 'Come on, Boys, hold him back. We'll learn him nay tae mess wi'a Macsnott.'

Burns was able to make a couple more direct scores before being overcome. The toilet smelt of rotting fish and there was a stickiness to the floor where he now lay which he hoped was only mud.

'Get them!' Picker shrilled.

Burns tensed, then groaned as his shoes were yanked off.

'No - not the lavvy hole - put them somewhere he canna get them,' shouted Picker as somebody went to put them down a toilet.

'Oh, right, I know where,' leered the shoe carrier and dashed outside.

Still holding Burns down, the gang looked to Picker for further instruction. There was a momentary silence as the pasty-faced bully dragged his sleeve over his nose. He searched in his pocket. Then he stepped forward.

The group fell back as if already distancing themselves. Still, Picker came on.

Burns had worried that his socks might get pulled off and they'd see that extra toe. He just knew Picker would make a big deal out of it, but then, in the pale gloom, something far far worse happened.

To his horror there came the brief flash of light on a blade. 🕷

20: A DISCOVERY

THE BOYS HAD LET GO OF BURNS. As he sprang up, an odd thing happened. A bagpipe tune started. But it was only inside his head. At first, the sound was distant; but quickly it grew, until all he could hear was its blast.

Long ago, pipers encouraged their troops into battle with their lusty playing. Burns could only think that a ghost of the McRae clan had come to do the same for him. Momentarily, he wondered if the same visited Rosie before she did her Cassowary stuff. Naturally, she wouldn't admit to any such thing, but the thought gave him courage. She always got a result!

By now, the piper was in full blast. The tune filled his heart, mind, made him feel a mile tall and so loud his voice boomed round the bleak lavvy walls, 'Put that away, Macsnott. I'm not afraid of that silly wee pen knife and I'm certainly not afraid of you.'

Picker's jaw dropped. His dream of a McRae begging for mercy died in an instant. By the look on some of the gang's faces, his leadership was vanishing too. This brat was tougher than the bully imagined.

'What's more,' continued Burns, the piper fairly dirling now, 'you're in plenty trouble already. Wait till Mr Caird hears you've been pretending to be the real paper boy.'

'Huh! That's no problem,' Picker sneered, waving the knife to and fro, 'I was just standing in for my cousin,'cos he asked me to.'

'At your age?' Burns scoffed, 'If Mr Caird hadn't had his specs broken, bet that was you, you'd never have got the chance.'

By now, the gang members were beginning to fidget. Spending all their playtime in a smelly toilet wasn't much fun. They started to edge towards the exit.

Unexpectedly and with a diabolical laugh, Picker struck.

The ghostly bagpipe tune stopped abruptly, the piper stole away and Burns was left with a pounding heart…and a ruined tie. Picker had cut it in half.

Now, holding up a clenched fist in triumph, he jeered, 'Ha ha! See how you get on with Old Crowbar with that. She fair hates seeing folk without a proper uniform and don't you bother telling on me either.' He thumb-jerked his chest proudly, 'Ah'm the main voice in the school choir an' the old Crowe knows it!'

Picker, slid his fingers through his greasy hair. He reckoned it'd been a good move. Whilst his pals were impressed by the act of destruction, he'd managed to get in the fact that he could also sing – a surprise bonus to a 'hard man' image. Also, McRae looked as if he'd had a good fright. He wasn't likely to meddle with him ever again.

Picker swaggered out, his troops following at a respectful distance.

Burns wanted to get away from this dismal place as well, but he was still a bit stunned. Anyway, he was stuck without shoes.

'I threw them onto the Heidie's flat roof,' the shoe-nicker had boasted and been congratulated by Picker for this act of courage.

Burns sighed. Climbing up on roofs meant even more trouble. Ruggabug! What a pain Picker was. As he leant against a wall, wondering what to do, there was a sound of light scurrying feet. A round face with huge freckles even bigger than Burns's ones peeped round the corner. It was wee Bobby.

'Are you Ok?' He asked, reassured nobody else was around. 'Yon Picker Macsnot's bumming round the playground he'd you begging for mercy.'

'A lotta lies,' Burns sounded weary, 'but he and his mates have taken away my shoes and look what they've done with my tie. Miss Crowe'll have a feejee.'

Bobby laughed. 'Och, that's easy. Just take it off. She hates folk speaking about fresh air. Just tell her, you canna breath with yours on, the classroom's so hot.' He spoke thoughtfully, 'and it is. It'd be great somebody else telling her that. But were you no scared with Picker?' He screwed up his face as if in actual pain.

Burns felt a bit better hearing Bobby's awed tones.

'Not really,' he said, 'if Picker hadn't had a knife there wouldn't have been an argument.'

'A knife?' Bobby threw a grubby hand to his mouth in horror.

In case Bobby suspected brain damage, Burns didn't mention pipers and went for a modest, 'Och, it was just a wee affair. It's my feet that are more of a problem.'

Bobby looked at his own as if they might have the answer. Then he said in reluctant way, 'If you'd like, you could take my shoes. You saved me in school today…' his voice trailed off.

Burns was touched by Bobby's gesture of friendship but, remembering the slippers explained about them, 'So maybe you could fish them out. I'd only need to wear them to get back to the classroom.'

He thought about his gym shoes. They lived in sweaty harmony with a tee shirt in a greasy bag inside his desk. It shouldn't be difficult to swap into them when Croweie wasn't looking. Still, he'd have to be careful, she was always saying she'd eyes in the back of her head.

A bitter wind blasting through a filthy broken window and banging the doors, made Burns shiver, but he took off his tie and made his shirt open-necked. Bobby eyed it with approval. 'Looks good.' Dimples showed as he added, ' and mind and say you're feeling breathless – she hates that.'

He'd returned with Andy who, proving kinsmanship handed over a Mars Bar. 'Kept it for you, Burns,' he said. His face, was as pink the slippers Bobby was now dangling with the triumph of a successful poacher.

'Oooh! Thanks, but what happened to your face?' Bruce asked, touched by his friend's sacrifice.

'Morag's gang caught and tied me to a tree. Seemed to think that bubblegum spread over your face makes you look really funny. Ach, girls! According to them catching boys's better'n doin' hand stands. I'd have got here sooner but for them.'

Burns was surprised. 'So where was Morag?'

'She'd been kept in for setting off a stink bomb. Wait till she hears what her gang's been up to.' Andy nodded at Bobby, 'and if he hadn't come along and freed me, I'd still be there Still, it couldn't be worser than what's been happening to you.' He pointed to the slippers. 'Jings! I never thought I'd see those again. How'll we get them past the old crow's nose?'

'Not to mention the back of her head,' Bobby said scrubbing his head hard to help him think.

'If we wait till everybody's back in school, then make a dash for it, nobody'll get a chance to see me. Once we're inside, you two go in together, and I'll sneak in close behind you.'

Burns sounded more positive than he felt. If this scheme should fail – No – he wouldn't think of it. Instead he thought about seven times eight which was just about as bad.

The boys waited for the going-in bell. When it went, they held out for a few nail biting moments until Bobby could stand it no longer. He popped his head round the door and reported, 'All clear.'

They tore out of the toilets and through the school entrance, skidding to a halt outside their classroom.

So far, Burns's plan had worked. No one had seen them. Now they were so near success, it only needed a degree of caution to join the class un-noticed.

Their luck stayed. Miss Crowe was bending down to pick up her pointer off the floor. Her pupils were so busy watching for a glimpse of her old fashioned grey knickers, nobody noticed the lads sidling in.

Burns carefully slipped on his gym shoes, hardly daring to breathe. He gave his pals the 'thumbs up' just as the teacher straightened up. She glared at the sniggering class.

'We'll have a little less laughter and a lot more work. Open your reading books.'

The children groaned inwardly, then prepared for a long slog until dinnertime whilst Burns, Andy and Bobby hid triumphant grins behind their hands.

Not only had Burns survived Picker, they'd just proved that Miss Crowe did not have eyes in the back of her head! 🐛

21: FUTURE PLANS

'**W**E HEARD ALL ABOUT YOU,' called Rosie. It was the end of the school day and she and Midge were at the school gate. They were waiting for Andy and Burns, bags trailing on the ground behind them, and trudging towards them.

As they reached them, Rosie, narrowed her eyes to look at her brother. He thought she'd the same look that the doctor had when his mother had taken him to have his hearing checked. He'd decided to play at being deaf, then, once in the surgery, he worried that he really was, with the doctor using fancy words he couldn't understand.

'Phew! Well at least we don't have to carry you home,' said Rosie, then, showing proper concern, slapped Burns heartily on the back. 'Och, don't look so down. There's no sweat about getting another tie. I've got a spare one. You should be grateful Picker went for that instead of anything else.'

'Delighted,' Burns squinted up at her through his fringe. 'Who needs to watch Dr Who when there's real scary stuff at school? ' He took the slippers out of his bag.

'There!' he slammed them into the rubbish bin with such force he nearly threw himself in as well.

A breathless Morag joined them. 'Sorted!' she said and wiped her hands as if pleased with a job well done, 'and guess what, Andy, the girls who tied you up are very very sorry and have promised me they won't do it again.'

Morag had obviously got her leadership back. Andy was impressed. 'Coo! How did you manage that?'

'Easy. I just told them that if Burns was found frozen with terror in the lavvy, it would be all their fault.'

Burns wished he could be as carefree as Morag now hopping over a crack in the pavement. He began to worry that he actually was a worrier. Still, he was glad that he was able to walk unaided, wasn't covered in blood, had faced up to Picker and had his shoes back thanks to Andy's climbing skills.

Midge heaved her schoolbag onto the other shoulder. 'Monday seems a lifetime away from Friday,' she smiled in a winning way at Burns, 'but at least we've something to look forward to.'

She was anxious in case he'd had enough of challenges. Desperate to go to Kate's Keep, she knew she'd better stay on good terms. Her continued kindly smile made him feel nervous and when she offered to carry his bag, he snapped, 'No! I'm fine. Able to walk'n everything.'

Oblivious to all but adventure Morag said, 'Midge – were you thinking about that treasure thingie?' Her skirt looked as if it might not last another day. Rosie wondered if she slept in it. Then, as Morag swung her schoolbag round her head, two buttons fell off her cardigan.

To avoid collateral damage, Rosie did a forward roll. Though graceful, it didn't stop her coming up covered in grime. Casually wiping her hands clean on her anorak so that its pale pink had a touch of brown, she said, 'We must have a meeting. What about tonight? We've lots to discuss.'

Everybody agreed it was a good idea and now that Burns reckoned Picker would leave him alone, he almost relaxed. He might even get back to being curious about the detector's find. He took a long suck at a sweetie Andy had given him, then said, 'After teatime, when you're ready, give us the towel – signal and we'll come to the hut.'

The tinned chicken soup and white bread showed Ma McRae's unique way of celebrating her family's return in good health. Not even homework was mentioned and when Morag arrived and looked blank when asked about the slippers, Ma didn't pursue the subject. Instead she said, 'Burns and Rosie are upstairs.'

The children, impatient, waited in Rosie's bedroom looking through the window for the towel signal from the Macduff house. As soon as it appeared, they charged downstairs, nearly knocking Mr McRae over. Reunited with his teeth, he spoke easily. 'I hope you guys aren't planning anything with the detector. Remember what Mr Muldoon said?'

'Yes, Da,' his children chorused whilst Morag fiddled with the remaining buttons on her cardigan, wriggled a bit and put on her wide-eyed innocence look.

Unmoved by her angelic expression, he added, 'And that goes for you too, Morag,'

Facing him direct she said, 'Don't worry, we're going nowhere with a detector.'

Brose, deciding a change of scenery might bring new bones to light, scampered after the children into the Macduff's garden. Since she'd had a little – just a little, tweak of his tail, she and Rat had some territorial issues about his shed. She hadn't liked the way he'd bared his teeth – didn't fancy his bite, but as soon as the children shut the shed door on her, she scratched frantically to get in.

'Now that everybody's here,' began Midge patting Brose's wriggling body absent-mindedly, 'we should make a list of what we'll need for Friday.' She fished out a notepad and pen from her trouser pocket and twitched her nose, a sure sign she was excited. 'All those in favour of going, say "Aye."'

On the chorus of 'Ayes,' Brose sat up and begged. Tucked behind the lawn mower, Rat glared. He wished they would all go and now. He hadn't finished his tea.

'Look! Brose's telling us she wants to come too,' laughed Burns who knew she was so clever she didn't have to go to school and could easily have written the list if she'd wanted to.

Andy spoke gravely. 'We'll need her. She can watch out for ghosts.'

Morag leant over Midge's shoulder. 'Don't forget torch.' She waited until this was done before adding, 'if I can get it off Dad of course.'

Midge's list grew long. Everybody thought up something different. Burns wasn't sure why they would need a rope but as they weren't allowed the detector and he'd run out of ideas, that was his contribution.

'String might be easier to carry,' Rosie suggested. 'Anyway we don't want to have to carry too much.'

'Ok,' said Burns delighted not to explain his suggestion whilst Midge pouted and threw the list away.

By now it was getting dark. The children hurried through their plans anxious to get home before the light went completely. Nobody seemed to think this odd whilst planning to be out in a pitch black Friday at midnight.

'It's good that we haven't been stopped going up Cloven Hill,' chuckled Rosie, 'but I bet our parents'd have a fejee if they knew what we're going to do.'

'Well, it's our secret, and sure they'll all be in bed by then,' Andy said. He turned to Morag. With his experience at the hands of her gang, unpleasantly fresh in his memory, he knew it was sensible keeping in with their leader. 'Me and Midge'll get up first and when it's time, we'll chuck wee stones at your window —let you know we've arrived.'

He was pleased when Morag, feeding potatoes into Mr Rat's home agreed.

'Do it on my window as well,' said Burns, 'and I'll tell Rosie.'

As the children parted, their heads buzzed with excitement.

'I can't wait,' said Rosie, 'It's so-o-o- exciting.'

'I so-o-o hope it doesn't end in disaster,' said Burns wondering if it was the weather or was he the only one with cold feet. 🐾

22: A NIGHT TIME ADVENTURE

BURNS AND ANDY had to recite The Braes of Cloven Hill at the end of the school term concert.

'You'll both just have to practise this poem at home,' Miss Crowe had said, handing the boys a sheet of paper. 'The last thing I've got,' she waved a hand round the classroom, 'is time.' She curled her nose as if she smelt something bad. 'It's supposed to be cheerful with a nice swing to it so I don't know how you'll get on. The pair of you look like a week of wet Sundays.'

The boys exchanged looks. If only she knew! Burns hadn't space in his head to worry about a bloomin' poem, his mind was so taken up fretting about Friday.

When it came, instead of the usual, 'Hurray - it's Frrri-day,' the children came home from school saying they were so tired, they needed an early night. This astonished their parents.

Ma McRae, mid pipe-drone mused to her husband, 'Poor dears. They must be exhausted. It's always the same this time of year.' To which Da McRae had sarcastically said, 'It's this time of year we get their school reports. I'm not surprised they're lying low.'

Whatever the thinking, lights were out in all the households earlier than usual. Whilst their children lay fully clad, hiding, wide eyed under their duvets the McRae parents fell blissfully asleep. Soon their snores could be heard bouncing against their wardrobe and even rattling the windows of their bedroom.

It made hearing outside noises difficult since it was also very windy and the ash tree branch was making a bid to get inside again. Burns, worried he'd miss Andy's alarm call, but then he heard the sharp sound of gravel crashing against his window and knew at once, the difference.

Still, it took courage to look out, and were those three darkly clad figures waving a torch, really his friends? They must be and judging by the wild arcs played it must be Morag holding the light and the one she promised she'd get. He risked switching on and off the light as the agreed signal, then crept though to Rosie.

'I know. I heard them. I think they must be throwing rocks,' she whispered, swinging her legs over the side of the bed and scrabbling round for her shoes. Brose came out of the toy cupboard and was immediately whisked up in Rosie's arms. Clamping her hand over Brose's mouth and pointy snout, she carried her downstairs.

The stairs creaked ominously at the last step but the McRae parents slept on. Burns, hurrying after his sister, closed the doors softly before racing towards the group.

 Glancing at their faces, Midge said, 'We forgot to blacken up too.'

'Well, I did my teeth, see?' Morag grinned and shone her torch on black tusks. 'Did them with soot. Gross taste tho'. She pulled a face making it an even more horrible sight.

'Yuck! But good for you, Morag,' Midge's excitement bubbled through the words. 'But we must go. Come on! Come on!' Her hair had escaped from its pigtails. It streamed across her face in a wind which tugged at the group like a child looking for attention. 'It's quite a gale but at least it's not raining.' She headed for the wall at the back of the McRae garden, then in an effortless leap was over it.

'Here…' she leant over to help the others. Brose, handed up by Rosie was first. As soon as she could, she started snuffling about some fallen leaves in such a normal way, it gave the children confidence. Everybody made it except Morag who was reluctant to give up her torch, even for a minute. She was carrying something else which clanked as she scrabbled about.

'Don't laugh,' Andy muttered as she continued an unsuccessful assault on the wall, 'but she's got her swords with her.' He sighed. 'She said she would and she has.'

Rosie gave a hysterical titter.

'Sssh!' Midge clamped a hand over her mouth. Then the moon came out from behind a cloud.

For a minute Burns was reminded of a lesson they'd had when Miss Crowe had given up on sums and explained similes to them.

She'd then said, 'Now give me an example of what you think the moon looks like, Bobby.'

'It's like a piece of shortbread with a bite taken out of it,' he offered.

'Tch! I suppose you have got 'like' in it but it's not very poetic.'

Bobby looked earnest. 'My Granny's dead now and she'll be in heaven. I think of her when I look up to the moon. She loved shortbread so I imagine her taking a bite out of it.'

Burns had been pleased that for once Miss Crowe had nothing more to say. Personally, looking up at the moon now, he hoped not to meet Bobby's granny quite yet. Anyway it was a full moon and more like a football and lit the way so well, Morag was able to pocket her torch. Helped by everybody's outstretched hands she joined the others.

To begin with, the children were so anxious the noise of their hurried rustling through the undergrowth of Cloven Hill would waken an entire Inverspurtle they only spoke in whispers and moved on tiptoe. But as they continued their upward climb, they began to relax.

'Gee whizz! I can't believe we're doing this,' said Andy, staying very close to Burns, 'Me an Midge thought we'd never get out of the house. Ma and Da kept asking us if we were all right or were we sickening for something. They'd never heard of us wanting to go to bed early - ever.'

'Well, mine are suffering from shock,' chuckled Morag. 'They went to bed even earlier than me and made my brother go too in case he was coming down with something serious. He was so-o annoyed.'

The way to Kate's Keep showed clear under the moon's cold light. As they walked along the wide path, the children kept together and in the middle. Lining trees, like threatening giants seemed to warn them that if they came near, they'd be hit or swallowed into their wind-tossed swaying branches. Between them, laurel bushes squatted like fat trolls, seeming to say in crackling whispers, 'You're strangers. You're not welcome. Stay away.'

Cloven Hill at night was less friendly than that sleeping giant during the day. An owl hooted, its cry eerie and lonely, whilst a rabbit shot past, its tail a brief alarm before it vanished.

Normally Brose would have given a joyful if hopeless chase, but now, she too stayed close. Her nails clicked on the hardened earth as disciplined as a marching soldier. Every now and then she'd look up enquiringly at her companions as if questioning their sanity. Her ears flapped in the wind whilst her cringing form showed how much she'd prefer being in bed with the Little Ponies. Yet, still, she plodded on - a worthy gang member.

'It's a good thing we've got Brose,' said Burns, 'she's so brave, she could take on anything - even a ghost - o-o-o-h!' He was cut off by a truly terrifying sight.

The moon had hidden behind a cloud and in the half light, they saw that Brose had changed into a wolf. 'Grrh!' With her hackles up, her body in the attack position, she looked twice her size. She feinted, reversed, snapped and growled with a sound so savage, it could have wakened the dead. And maybe she had.

'My Lord!' gasped Rosie, putting her hand cold as ice, into Burns's one. 'Look! There.' 🦋

23: COURAGE NEEDED

FEAR PARALYSED EVERYBODY as they saw what had so terrified Brose. It was something high up: white and misshapen. Even scarier was the way it moved to and fro whispering with a sound as if speaking directly to each one.

'Morag, shine a light,' Midge hissed but Morag was so caught up with her swords, her hands were full.

Then Brose broke free. She bounded forward, continuing to growl and snap. The children, still hypnotised by the glimmering, swaying, rustling movement now had their fear doubled. Brose was putting her life at risk for them. Burns felt cold sweat break out on his forehead.

He forced a croak, 'Here, Brose,' whilst Morag managed at last to get to and switch on her torch. Uncertainly, she played its beam on the ghoulish shape. The light seemed to magnify threatening shapes everywhere but as the wind sobbed and tore at their clothes, the children suddenly felt relief wash over them.

It was only an old polythene sheet. Towel-sized, it was caught, high up in the tree branches. The wind, now reaching a frenzy, whipped it as if desperate to free it. It seemed to the children that the sheet was rustling back in defiance.

'Good old Brose, you got a fright too,' laughed Morag. She flashed her torch to and fro then, cupping her hand to foghorn her voice, she cried, 'O.K. Kate's Keep - here we come!'

'Wait! We need to put Brose on the lead. We don't want her trying to save us again.' Rosie searched in her pocket. 'Look, we needed string after all. Good job I brought some.'

Holding the dog so she got tied, Burns smiled to himself. What a good thing he'd suggested rope for Midge's list.

Once more, the moon came out. Under its steady gaze, the children travelled on in a lighter mood.

Andy, chewing hard and in the way of someone with bubble-gum losing its flavour, said longingly, 'That moon's like a smartie in my mouth.'

'More like a disco ball at a disco,' said Rosie giving a little jig. Burns wondered if she felt brave enough to do a handstand, but they were now nearing the top and the path was easing into a gentle slope. When Kate's Keep came into view, it made for an easy saunter.

Midge loped forward, pushing back her fringe to see better. 'It looks much bigger and blacker, doesn't it.' Her smile was sly. 'Wooh!' came a banshee howl. The sound bounced back as if mocking them.

'Don't!' Andy hit his sister whilst Morag advanced with a sword. Rosie who had gone back to walking normally, snapped, 'Midge, with your hair all over the place, you're like Medusa.'

'Who's Medusa?' asked Andy.

'A wifie with snakes for hair,' said Burns. 'Don't you remember Crowie telling us about her in the days even before she was a teacher.' He couldn't imagine such a time but she'd shown them a book. It had a picture of Medusa inside and said Greek Mythology on the outside. Not even Crowie was that old.

Midge didn't like the way the conversation was going. Any minute now she might be branded as being a not-nice person. Catching her hair back and stuffing it down the back of her jersey she said, 'Ok, ok, I'm sorry. Can't you take a joke? Now where's the famous tree you were telling us about?'

'There!' pointed Andy. 'Look, it's obvious.'

The picnic area had been transformed into a magical place with stars for a ceiling and the moon a silvering globe. Rosie whispered, 'I feel as if we're the only folk alive in Inverspurtle.' Then, taking in the deep shadows, dark as black velvet surrounding it. 'Let's stay close.'

The wobble in her voice pleased Burns. She might be his big sister but maybe not as big as she thought.

Still the wind blew hard, but here, the leaves on the surrounding trees danced, whispering in a gentle chorus. Only the small and stunted rowan tree, stayed still. Burns remembered times when he'd been the one left out from play. The tree looked as desolate as he'd then felt.

'Looks dead to me,' sniffed Midge.

Burns wanted to defend the tree. He stroked the trunk. 'That's what you think. It's alive alright.'

He knelt down and started to scrape away the earth he and Andy had previously disturbed. 'Come on Morag, shine your torch. Let's hope

Big George hasn't gone off with that box.'

The others moved quickly to help. Their fingers searched frantically feeling the earth, cold and clammy. Occasionally a sharp pebble would trick them into thinking they'd found something, then, just as Morag was beginning to fiddle with the torch and not shine it very helpfully, and Rosie was feeling a handstand coming on, Burns gave a great shout.

'I've found. I've found it. Look!'

He drew out a small metal box, and with trembling fingers, put it gently on the ground. The children gathered round in an excited huddle and gazed at it. It looked ancient. For a moment, there was silence as each wondered what on earth could it be and had it anything inside. 🐛

24: KATE

ANDY BROKE THE SILENCE. He couldn't help it. Jumping up and down, and popping bubblegum, he burst out, 'I want to open it. Oh, please, please. I asked first.'

Burns was more cautious. 'Wait! It might hold some terrible disease. Remember Crowie telling us about the Black Death?'

Rosie was exasperated, 'Honestly, Burns. All you remember is gloom and doom. If you're so bloomin' anxious, you should just go home.'

'I was just saying...' Burns protested, 'we'll be sorry if we all die.' He lapsed into a hurt silence whilst Morag played her torch over the box. 'Go on, Andy,' she said, 'live the fear! Look, you can use one of my swords to open it. That way you can keep your distance.' She thrust one at Andy who took it gingerly. 'See! It's a good thing I took them.' She was smug.

'Yeh – but why two?' Midge, looking on critically, scrubbed her nose hard. 'I don't remember them going on the list.'

Morag was saved from answering as using the sword tip, Andy easily prised the box open. The children craned forward whilst he lifted out a small scroll of paper.

Midge used her height to lift it from her brother, 'Take care or you'll tear it,' then seeing everybody's grasping hands, she held it aloft saying, 'Calm down, you guys. You could easily rip it in half.'

Now the moon was shining so brightly she hardly needed Morag's torch. Still she took a little time peering at paper so old, it looked as if it had been steeped in tea. There was writing on it but the ink was faded.

As she started to read, strands of her hair escaped. They played about her face as she began to speak in a hesitant voice unlike her own.

Indicted o the cryme o Witchcraft ↲ Kate Macpherson hav bin sairly wranged. Prove wil cam when a rodden Tree blooms quhar this Kist is foond an ↲ met muckle mischanter.

X

William Haggerty. Clerk. 1703

Her voice tailed away as she looked up. The paper shook in her hand and though she wore enough warm clothing, she was shivering, her face a white mask in the moonlight. At length she said, 'Poor Kate. She must've had somebody to write this for her. Look, that 'x' must be her mark.'

Uncertainly, the others gathered about her in a pool of light encircled by darkness. For a while, the children just gazed at the letter. The comforting sound of the wind moving the leaves continued. But then it died away, leaving a terrible quiet. It was as if everything and everywhere was holding its breath.

Suddenly, there was a blood curdling, spine chilling howl. It was Brose. No longer brave and with a cry so awful, it gripped each child with a terror as great as that of the dog. Had Rosie not been holding onto her lead, she'd have broken free. As it was, she strained on it, moaning piteously. The branches on the trees now writhed as if in mortal agony and this was especially terrifying for there yet came no sound from them. Only Brose's distress broke the silence.

No sooner had everyone began to move from shock to think of flight than an even more frightful noise rent the air and stopped them. It was as if all the sounds of anguish, despair, pain and fear had been rolled into one terrible cacophony.

Deafened, all the children dived to the ground. Holding their ears and trying to block out that awful sound, they crouched there, despaired of ever escaping from that noise trapped in its pool of light. It seemed to go on forever but at last Brose tugged free, her movement, seeming to release the children from their frozen state.

Burns was first to get up. He grabbed the swords, their cool touch reassuring him. Making a shape of the cross, he raised them and with a cry louder even than all around him, shouted, 'Kate! Go! Rest in peace.'

In days to come, all the children agreed that the sweetest sound in the world had been the return of the wind sighing in the trees. The dreadful din which had so terrified them, had died away at Burns's words.

Now, their only concern was to put as much distance between them and here as possible. Brose was back, fully recovered but Rosie grasped hold of her as if she'd never let her go again. But just as they turned for home, Morag's hair despite the lack of sugar, stood on end.

'The rowan tree!' she croaked, 'Look!'

Despite the pain risk, Burns actually pinched himself whilst the others stared at it. Surely the bright red berries hanging from a now graceful and very much alive rowan tree must be a dream!

'It's a miracle,' Andy said. He clasped his hands and bowed his head.

'It's what Kate prophesied,' whispered Midge. 'Now it's up to us to clear her name. Wait till we show our parents and tell them about rowans in April.'

Burns's familiar worry-mode had returned. 'What'll they say to us – and what about Big George Munro? Ruggabug! He'll have a feejee if he hears we've been back to Kate's Keep.' He nibbled his knuckle. The taste was so horrible he wondered why people bit their nails.

'Well, we didn't use the metal detector, did we?' retorted Morag, 'Let's head home. I've had enough for one night. Here, instead of being such an old fuss spot, you carry the swords, Burns.' She raced off down the hill running so fast the light from her torch looked like a shooting star.

25: SHARING NEWS

WAKING TO SUNSHINE leaking through the curtains and checking all his limbs were in place, Burns was surprised. Racing home last night, everybody'd agreed they'd never sleep. But as soon as he and Rosie had stolen back into their house, he'd fallen into bed as if unconscious.

'Hey! It's a bonny morning. You awake, Burns?' Rosie called from her room.

'I'm coming through.' Burns hurried out of bed, hopping over the usual pile of clothes and doing the same in Rosies. 'I'm wondering if we should tell Ma and Da about last night.'

'No! We've agreed to leave it to the others.' Rosie punched her pillows, then snuggled down under her duvet. Brose popped her head out from her usual nest, checked around, seized a stray Little Pony, then apparently having had enough adventures, retired again.

'I think Midge's idea to tell our folk is ace,' said Rosie.

Burns idly turned the heap of clothes with his foot. 'What if we get a row?'

'They won't get half what we'd get if it was us telling them.' Rosie put her arms behind her head and gazed dreamily up at the ceiling, 'but what a night that was. I can hardly believe it happened. Can you?'

'No and what if there's worse to come? We might be grounded forever. Maybe we shouldn't let Andy and Midge say anything.'

'What? Not on your Nelly!' Rosie sat bolt upright. 'We owe it to Kate to tell the world she wasn't a witch. Come on, Burns. I'm beginning to think you really are a worrier.'

'No, I'm not. But if we get the works, it'll all be your fault.' Burns picked up a piece of Inverspurtle Rock sticking to Rosie's duvet, ate it and felt better. 'but if you're sure…'

'Look, it'll be fine. Anyway, aren't you not just dying to see the box and the letter again? Midge promised she an Andy'd take them along with Morag.' Rosie looked at her clock. 'And look at the time! They'll be here any minute.'

The McRaes had just finished breakfast when the trio arrived. Mr McRae, Inverspurtle Journal under his arm, was just about to head for his bath when Morag blocked his way.

With a huge smile she said, 'We've something really exciting to tell you.'

'Oh yes?' He sounded anxious. Mr McRae did not associate Morag with improvement.

Morag's smile moved into cherubic mode as she pushed Midge forward. 'Well – Midge has.'

Poor Midge went rather red, then rather white, twitched her nose then, encouraged by further shoving by Morag, began.

That morning, Da McRae was to learn that the 'Inverspurtle' would never again produce the same level of excitement as Kate's scroll. Mrs McRae was equally enthralled, seemingly oblivious to the increasing, burning smell coming from the kitchen.

'It's all true,' Burns tugged at his father's sleeve. 'and if you don't believe us, come on up to Kate's Keep and you'll see for yourself.'

'It's some tale, kids,' Mr McRae threw away his newspaper, 'but why tell us and not your own parents? I'm sure they'd love to know.'

'We thought you'd be best,' Morag said cheerfully. 'Anyway, my folk don't really know what I've been up to. They're just getting over my smell game.'

Everybody laughed except Andy who was sure Mrs McRae would make a connection between Morag's game and the burning smell from her kitchen. Worse, she might offer what was being incinerated, all round. He scampered to the door. 'Oh, let's go now. I'm dying to see yon tree in the daylight.'

He swung the door to and fro' making a draught. It blew the burning smell throughout the house.

'My bannocks!' gasped Mrs McRae.

'Come on, come on,' pleaded Andy, 'You can catch up with us later, Mrs McRae.' Then he raced off shouting, 'Last one up the Hill's a hairy kipper.'

When she did get away, Mrs Mcsporran just caught up after everybody reached Kate's Keep. They'd been arguing about who'd be last so they were especially pleased to see her.

She didn't seem to mind being a hairy kipper whilst her husband was more concerned that he hadn't changed out of his pyjamas. But he forgot all that when he saw the tree.

'That's incredible,' he murmured, 'and those berries look as if they've been polished. I'll bet Big George Muldoon'll get a shock when he sees this.' Seeing the children's sniggers, he said hurriedly, 'What I mean is Mr Muldoon.'

'Speaking of which,' whispered his wife pointing to a bulky figure appearing. With his mouth open and eyes popping there was little doubt. Big George was amazed.

Burns nipped behind his father whilst the others watched on uncertainly. How would he react?

Momentarily they thought that Mr McRae in pyjamas was the reason for Big George shaking his head, but when he said, 'I don't understand it. It's like a young tree. As for the berries – they're like a sign of something,' they breathed again.

'And that's just what they are,' chorused the children and gathered round him. Then they retold the fantastic story. Mr and Mrs McRae were interested to hear it again too since everybody chipped in with their own particular act of bravery Midge hadn't apparently thought important enough to include.

Burns had worried he might lose the box and letter but trusted Andy who'd taken charge of them swearing he would guard them with his life.

'And look – here's they are.' He showed them to Big George.

He'd gone speechless making Mrs McRae worry she'd have to give him The Kiss Of Life. After a bit of back slapping and loosening his braces, however, he managed, 'This is the biggest thing since Inverspurtle Thistle beat Foggy United a century ago.' His smile became so big and cheery, he was almost unrecognisable. 'It's a real something for our museum. The curator just has to see this.'

'Lead the way then, Big George!' yelled Morag in a forgetful moment, and then to everyone's surprise including her own, blushed. Big George, however, with one more lingering look at the rowan tree, appeared not to notice. Apart from Mr McRae who wanted to get properly dressed, everybody else followed Big George speeding for Inverspurtle.

The museum curator was surprised to see so many people so early in the morning, but she began to see why when shown the box and letter.

'I think you've unearthed an old tinder box,' she said. 'People used them to start fires before the days of matches. It's a real find.' She smiled at the group who, once more told their tale. 'As for the letter,' she held it up to the light, 'it seems genuine enough. Of course we'll have to have it checked, but right now,' her eyes gleamed with excitement, 'I'd almost swear it's authentic and of huge local interest.'

Everybody agreed it would be best to leave the curator in charge of the finds and delighted when she said that whilst the museum would love to exhibit the box, the letter could be displayed at Kate's Keep.

'We don't know how long the rowans will last, but folk can come and see the tree for a very long time. We'll write a piece about how it was found, and of course, we'll include the story of you and your find.' She looked approvingly at the children. 'Would you like that?'

'I'd rather be allowed to the top of the tower on my own,' murmured Burns.

When his father's fear of heights was explained, the curator looked at Big George, 'I'm sure that could be arranged. And maybe a plaque at Kate's Keep?'

'Of course. Nay bother.' Big George couldn't have sounded happier. 'Now I'm off to the Inverspurtle Journal to tell them about the tree. It's going to be a real crowd puller – and d'you know what? The more people there are around the hill, the less chance there'll be of vandals.'

'Very true and guess what,' Mrs McRae looked straight at Andy. 'It's time to go home. You must all be hungry and I've done some baking. It's a wee bit over cooked but if you nibble off the edges, I'm sure the middle will be fine.'

Balking at the prospect, Midge, even, was fast. 'Now that we've solved the Cloven Hill secret we need to get home and tell our own parents.' Seeing Ma McRae's disappointment, she quickly added, 'but we wanted you to know first.'

'Oh well,' Ma sighed, 'if you must. It's probably time for some peace and quiet. You'll surely have had enough excitement for a while. Little did she know! 🌿

26: AND FINALLY

O N THE NIGHT OF THE CONCERT, the school hall was packed
with parents, pupils and Inverspurtle folk. They were all
curious to see the kids who'd put their town on the map.
No longer was it a sleepy wee place. There'd been telly crews, world-
wide newspaper coverage and enough visitors flocking there to gain it
the 'Most Favourite Spot in Scotland Award.' Already, the Inverspurtle
Highland games organisers were over whelmed by the number of sport
enthusiasts, keen to see Kate's testimony and the rowan tree as well.

Finally explaining about her father's nine toes, Morag said, 'Dad
dropped a hammer on one – mashed it to pieces an' he doesn't want
to lose another, so he's volunteering to be the safety officer for the
Throwing the Hammer event.'

Sitting in the audience beside Bobby's parents, Mr McRae said, 'It's all
very exciting, but I think I'm going to have to take over the cooking
from my wife, the pipe band's so busy.'

Mrs McRae sighed, 'I suppose it's the price of fame.' She looked
disappointed but cheered up when Mrs Dickie said, 'Yes, Bobby heard
you. Says he saw the band play outside. It so inspired him, he wants to
learn. We think it might even help him with his breathing as well.' She
nodded to Miss Crowe overseeing the front area of the hall set aside
for pupils, 'It's not been easy for him. Let's hope their new teacher
recognises somebody suffering from asthma.'

The hall buzzed with excitement. Backstage, tossing her pigtail back
and twitching her nose, Midge said, 'Can you believe the crowd? I'm
sick at the thought of facing them. I haven't even eaten all day and I'm
sure I'm going to forget my words.'

Burns couldn't reply. He was too busy trying to remember his own
ones and using soap to plaster down his fringe. He'd been pulling on
it in the hope it would cover at least half his face. Beside him, Andy
popped gum. He too was nervous.

Midge's anxiety went as soon as she stepped on stage. To a roar of
applause, she managed to keep everything under control to triumph
through her piece.

'Lucky Midge, that's her turn, over,' Rosie said, 'I bet she's starving now.'
She caught her class teacher beckoning to her. 'Ooh, it's my turn now. I'm shaking, see?' She twiddled her fingers then dashed off.

'You'd think she'd have stage fright,' said Andy watching a gymnastic display that rocked the hall and brought cheering people to their feet. 'I just hope she doesn't run out of space. She's really fit.'

'Aye. It's all that forward rolls and handstand stuff,' sighed Burns, 'She spends her life upside down. Can't see the fun of it, myself. Mind you with all this running about I think I'm getting pretty fit myself. But, come on, Andy, we'll be on soon. Ruggabug!'

By now, the audience was on fire. To the boys' delight, many in the audience knew the words of their poem and joined in. Surprised into confidence, Burns pushed his fringe to the side to see out. Someone shouted, 'Brilliant! Now we all know what our local heroes look like.'

Dazed and delighted, the boys stumbled off. They joined Midge and Rosie who were with the other children, who'd already performed. Miss Crowe, poker-prod in hand, ensured sweetie rustling and chat was kept to a minimum.

'It's Morag's turn but she said not to keep a place for her, she's staying backstage afterwards.' Rosie nodded as their friend appeared on stage. 'Judging by the squeals coming from there, what d'you bet she's been using her swords already.'

They looked harmless enough. When she came on stage and danced over them her parents had to remind themselves that the sprite in the Og tartan frill with the soot-free smile actually was their daughter. There was an encore. But, despite all appeals, Morag didn't come back.

The concert continued. The headmistress had never seen or heard such an appreciative audience but at last it was time for the final performance.

She rose, thanked the public, parents and performers, eyeballed those at the front numbering most of the school and beginning to get restless, then announced the school choir would round off the evening.

'We are very lucky to have such a fine group of singers. Of course, we have our music teacher to thank for the high standard they manage to achieve.'

There was a polite ripple of applause. The music teacher showed her teeth and shuffled her music papers with the expertise of a card player. As she dashed behind the stage curtains there issued some pretty unmelodic noises.

Picker Macsnot had been given a chair as centre point. As the choir milled about him finding a place, he felt like a king sitting amongst his servants. 'You'll stay sitting until it's your spot,' the music teacher had said. This made him even more big-headed and when young Morag Og came clanking towards him with her swords, he commanded her to kneel before him.

Somewhat to his surprise, she'd replied, 'Certainly your Majesty.' She crawled round his chair. 'Your uniform needs a wee tidy,' she said and fiddled about a bit.

Picker felt a small tug on his trousers then forgot it as, backing out, his new slave gave a dazzling smile and said, 'And the best of luck, Your Highness.'

This nearly caused a riot amongst the others and annoyed the music teacher no end. Picker however, loved it. He puffed his chest with pride. He couldn't wait for the curtains to be raised.

Meanwhile the headmistress was holding forth about school funds and would everybody bear the scarcity of them in mind when passing the collection boxes on their way out.

She continued, 'I realise I've forgotten to mention our singer carrying the responsibility of solo part this evening. I'm sure we can rely on young Master Macsnot not to disappoint us. I know his fine singing gift will please us all.'

Led by Bobby Dickie, the words were drowned out by a burst of raspberry blowing noises from the front. Miss Crowe gave a 'shish' with as much venom as five cobras. To cheer her up she thought about Picker's knife lying in her handbag. She'd found him with it. 'That should be confiscated. Give it to me that at once,' she'd said, and popped it in her handbag. It would come in handy for pruning her thistles when she retired.

'And now!' The headmistress swept her arms and the curtains opened. 'Let's give a warm welcome to The School Choir!'

Every parent who'd children in it immediately searched them out, to the exclusion of anybody else. As singing filled the room, it made sentimental listeners reach for their hankies. It reminded them of happy times when they too were young.

Now, at last, it was Picker's moment. Seated in his chair, he'd everybody's attention. Lights were dimmed. He was spot lit. There was complete silence. He'd lost some grip over his gang since the toilet affair. This performance should restore it. He checked on members of his group. They were gazing up at him from rows where they'd been planted to ensure a rapturous applause.

With him being the only one now visible, power coursed through him. This had to be his finest hour.

Bruce nudged Andy. 'How did that cat get here?'

'What cat?' Andy looked around.

'There!' Bruce, seeing it at Picker's feet, caught it looking straight back at him.

'I can't see anything,' said Andy.

Bruce felt a prickling at the back of his neck. Was he the only one to see this cat? Looking back on previous sightings, he remembered it went with bad happenings. But then, remembering how he and his friends had overcome them all, he relaxed. They'd learnt to cope with just about anything and with a bit of luck, this cat might mean bad luck for someone else. He rubbed his eyes, and looked, then looked again.

He could now only see Picker who was taking a deep breath and puffing out his chest before he stood up.

Then, to the bully's horror, and everlasting shame, there was pandemonium. The hall rocked as the audience erupted into laughter, because… guess what…

HIS TROUSERS FELL DOWN!

103 PTO

October 2015

Dear Reader

We hope you've liked our book. Now that it's finished, Jane says she'll miss us but we've given her great memories. Not all our ideas and words have been used but here's some we'd like to see in print.

Taken from a pupil's story. 'MIDNIGHT HOUR ADVENTURE'

> Burns and Andy put new batteries in their torches in case the existing batteries conked out.

> …they walked up the hill and could smell damp, misty air and see shadows prancing around the trees and they could hear the hooting of an owl. They thought it was scary.

> …He said to himself, "I want that box."

We were asked what we thought the moon looked like.

> It's a beautiful smile.

> A gold penny in my purse.

> A golf ball in the hole.

> A white ball in the night.

> A blue jewel on a dark blue cloth.

> A Gruyere cheese in a box.

> A white fish and it swims in the sea.

> A rock face in the sky.

> A diamond in black paint.

We weren't asked to describe Mr Sleaford but Jane saw this, liked it and sneaked it in. Ssh! Don't tell him!

He's like a massive sweet gingerbread man. He has a gingerbread house. He is the one who makes the sun.

So what was scratching on Burns's bedroom window? (See if you can find any matching illustrations in our book.)

Some answers.

A ruggabug monster with fluffy hair, short thick legs, long thin arms, big eyes and an angry mouth.

A monster with a red tail and horns.

An owl

A monster with wings, human hands, hairy ears and breathing fire.

A lonely animal escaped from a wild life park.